356

DATE DUE

8 Jan '59 MS	7 May '59 G
13 Jan '59 KF	19 Feb '63 ✓
12 Feb '59 MS	
13 Feb '59 G	
25 Feb '59 G	0 8 FEB 70 COL
17 Mar '59 MS	
27 Mar '59 MS	
17 Apr '59 MS	
29 Apr '59 G	
14 Nov '60 MS	

10/27/60 Reserve Room

A DANGEROUS WOMAN

And Other Short Stories

By JAMES T. FARRELL

●

An outrageous spoof, followed by a bitterly ironic story of a writer to whom success came too quickly and too easily; painfully humorous adolescents set against their even more absurd elders; a tragic tale of a brilliant Negro student; another of a wistful Irish girl in London—such the stories in this new collection by James T. Farrell. The scenes change—we are in Paris, in Switzerland, in Washington, with Polish exiles in New York, and finally back in Chicago—at a high-school dance, then among express-company employes.

But, whatever the scene and whatever the tone of the story, it is the human entities that count; here is a writer who, no matter how far his interests range nor how widely he travels, concentrates his attention not on rocks and rills nor on trees and templed hills but on the men and women, the girls and boys of the neighborhood, whether of the Left Bank or the South Side.

As the Boston Herald said of Mr. Farrell's OMNIBUS OF SHORT STORIES: "If any writer has covered the human scene with more perception and more sympathy, it would be hard to place him,"—and this new volume proves again that Mr. Farrell, as always, writes with a unique understanding and sympathy for his fellow men.

A Dangerous Woman

JAMES T. FARRELL

A Dangerous Woman

and other stories

NEW YORK
THE VANGUARD PRESS, INC.

to Virginia and Robert Livingston

Since brass, nor stone, nor earth, nor boundless seas,
But sad mortality o'er sways their power.

Shakespeare

Contents

A Dangerous Woman

She stood out among the few women at the cocktail party. More striking than beautiful, she was dark-haired and her black eyes burned with intense absorption.

I happened to notice her before she spoke to me and I had an impression of her wandering through a crowd of men, either lost or a bit drunk. On seeing her, I immediately thought of Oliver Hartwell, a gay and highly intelligent American trade unionist who had arrived in Stockholm two days before the party. Several of us had preceded him there, and besides discussing politics and the cold war, we had also lightly warned him not to let a Swedish woman get her hooks into him, and he had bantered with us. He was in a corner of the large room and had not noticed this woman.

Wearing a well-fitting and expensive black dress, she moved about aimlessly and restlessly. I speculated about her, not so much because she was attractive but rather on account of her burning eyes and her round and pretty face which wore such a vague and dislocated expression. Was she trying to put the hooks into one of us, I wondered? But even though I was alone and am as attracted to pretty women as any man, I found myself not interested in her in any amorous or sexual sense. I stood in a corner watching her, wondering about her, but I didn't approach this Swedish woman. I was not afraid of the hooks being sunken into me nor was I restrained by shyness. I had been almost instantly struck by something strange in her. I knew that she wasn't a woman to flirt with. Those eyes, that face wrapped in surly sadness, her careless and graceless posture, her movements so unlike those of a woman

9

with a fine and well-formed figure, all this put me on guard.

It was a semi-official party given by a friend of mine, Ray Jackson, who held a high diplomatic rank. This was not the first such affair that I had attended in Stockholm, and I had come to realize that these parties followed a pattern. There were more men than women present, and the Swedish men at first acted very stiffly. They stood about drinking cocktails and saying little. When they were introduced to you, many of them clicked their heels together, bowed and said in English, "Thank you." Slowly and gradually, they thawed, thanks to two or three cocktails. At first, conversation was very polite and formal. Then it usually turned to politics, especially Swedish politics or else to Swedish attitudes in relationship to the Cold War and America. And the Swedish politicians or trade officials present would most frequently respond to questions with one or two set answers. They would say that the question asked was a very difficult one and that, also, it was not a Swedish question. Only gradually might the conversation become more interesting. And in the meantime, the Americans present had picked out the available good-looking women and flirted with them. The Swedish men talked among themselves or with the Americans who had not found a woman to flirt with.

This party was proceeding according to pattern. The thawing-out had begun. The noise of conversation was rising, and the few attractive women were receiving attention from the Americans. But this particular woman moved through the crowd in her black silk dress, lost.

She approached me and said that her name was Mrs. Helga Svenson. The name registered because my host, Ray, had mentioned her husband: he was one of the most important men in the country, politically. Then, noticing the glass of orange juice which I held, she said: "I am surprised that an author like you is drinking that."

Her English was excellent, but her voice was quite thick. I assumed immediately that she was drunk. I joked about my orange juice, saying that it was so potent that I feared I couldn't take another and stay sober.

"I belong to the Society for the Elimination of Restrictions on Alcohol," she told me rather challengingly.

We talked for a few minutes. She seemed offensive to me, so I parried her remarks about drinking and alcohol and remained aloof. But suddenly I realized that she wasn't drunk, as I had believed, and that she had something on her mind. In the meantime, some of the guests had left, and others were leaving.

"I'm surprised that you are not drinking."

I shrugged my shoulders.

"I belong to the Society for the Elimination of Restrictions on Alcohol," she repeated. "What do you think of that?"

"I have no opinion about it. I know nothing about the situation here," I answered, again shrugging.

"Why are you not drinking?"

"When I drank, I didn't always handle it well, so I quit."

"Alcohol is rationed here, but I am fighting this. Don't you like to enjoy yourself? What do you do?"

She continued talking in this manner, but I responded only with noncommittal or irrevelant replies. She seemed too insistent and aggressive. But I became convinced that she had something on her mind and that she wanted to talk about it.

A moment later, I excused myself. By this time, almost all of the guests had gone. Mrs. Helga Svenson stood in a corner, staring about with anger in eyes that should have been beautiful, inviting and seductive. She gazed across the large room as if she were staring at nothing and as though the men remaining in the room were not visible to her. Then she again began to walk about aimlessly. I dropped down on the sofa, alone. I didn't look at her, but then—suddenly—it occurred to me that in some way she really wanted to unburden herself. And just then my host, Ray, happened to pass in front of me and I suggested that he invite Mrs. Svenson to remain for dinner. He did.

Mrs. Svenson sat at one end of the sofa, surrounded by six of us men. The five other men were trade unionists,

including my host who had been in the trade union move-
ment in America before he had gone into the government
service. Cocktails were being drunk while dinner was
being prepared.

Mrs. Svenson looked into her glass and curled her lips
with bitter amusement.

"I am a member of the Society for the Elimination of
Restrictions on Alcohol." Her voice was dry but a bit
thick.

While a gay surprised laugh greeted her remark, Oliver
lifted his glass and said: "Success to your work—*Skoal.*"

"I don't care if my work is successful or if it isn't," she
said challengingly.

"Why work for it then?" I asked.

"I'm not really interested in my work," she said dully.

"Why do you do it then?" Oliver asked.

"I must have something. I must have something to do."

"It's a worthy cause," one of the trade unionists joked.

"I can't stay home and do nothing. If I stay home with
nothing to do, I'll go crazy," she went on. "But I don't
care about eliminating restrictions on alcohol. If *men*
want to get drunk . . ." She shrugged her shoulders. "If
men want to get drunk . . ." She pronounced "men" with
intense anger almost with venom.

"You work in a good cause," someone said.

Mrs. Svenson smiled quite enigmatically. "There is only
one cause," she said.

"What's that?" someone asked.

"Woman—to make woman free."

"Aren't women free in Sweden?" Oliver Hartwell asked.

"American women," she answered, "have washing machines, vacuum cleaners. They are free of drudgery. . . .
We're not. We are not. We are not free." She became
intense. "And unless they let us be free, we will revenge
ourselves. We will get our revenge." She paused and then
she spoke with even more intensity. "We will destroy
their sons."

She glared at us, from one to the other, and an enig-
matic smile came back to play upon her face. But her
words had struck no spark; no one in the room was
shocked by her angry words. I, personally, was sad rather

than disturbed to hear her speak this way. If she had made Oliver or the others uneasy they did not reveal it.

Oliver Hartwell began asking her questions about freedom and working conditions for women in Sweden. He described versions of the efforts made and the successes achieved by American trade unions to improve working conditions for women and to attain equal pay for equal work. And he explained some of our laws protecting women and making it illegal for them to be employed to perform certain kinds of heavy labor as, for instance, mine work. Mrs. Svenson objected to such laws, contending that if women were not allowed to do the same labor as men, they were then not being treated as equals. An argument followed. Mrs. Svenson disagreed with Oliver and the other trade unionists concerning the value of protecting women in industry. She insisted that if women were not allowed to do the same work as men, it meant that they were being treated and regarded as unequal and inferior.

"She has a Soviet attitude toward women," Oliver said in the midst of the discussion.

"No, I have not," she insisted. "Men do not treat us as equals. And if they don't—we will destroy their sons."

She looked at us, intently and with flashing but uncertain eyes.

Considered in terms of the conditions of her country, the circumstances of Helga Svenson's life were very favorable. I had seen some apartments in Stockholm and, though these were clean and modern, they were quite small. But judging from what she said, it was quite clear that her home was larger than average. Also she had a garden. And socially she moved in the highest circles in the country.

Further—and we were all certain of this—she had never spoken to men as she was speaking to us. I had heard much of the complaints of Swedish women against men, and I was hearing directly what I had already been told about. Helga had restrained none of her feelings. And as she continued to talk with us while we waited for dinner, her voice registered ranges of intensity, passion and anger. Her features remained set, almost expressionless, as though fixed in a mask. But now and then, at odd moments, this would all change and she would smile apologetically.

There was more discussion dealing with working conditions and wage rates for women in various countries. Helga lost all interest in this subject and sat looking about dully and bored. She grudgingly denied that her attitude on women was the same as the Soviet one. But she finally acknowledged that perhaps pregnant women shouldn't be allowed to work close to the time that they would give birth, and that it wasn't good for women, even when not pregnant, to have to do manual labor. Then she said, changing the subject of discussion: "My work does not interest me in the slightest. But I couldn't stay home all day and merely do housework. I couldn't stand my son. He's two and a half years. I couldn't stand him. I screamed at him every day. I couldn't bear doing housework, cleaning up dirt."

"Who takes care of your son?" I asked.

"I have a maid."

"You're not as badly off as you think," I told her.

Oliver Hartwell gave me a critical gaze for having said this. He later reprimanded me for many of the questions I asked Mrs. Svenson. However, I had believed that I sensed a desire on her part to speak about the matters contained in my questions and, also, I could only be interested in her psychologically.

"I was screaming at my son all of the time," she said. "I was quarreling, fighting with myself. Now I get along better with him. He's happier too. I can come home from my work and kiss him and not be angry."

At this point, a sad mood came over me. I had encountered women like Mrs. Svenson before. I thought of her caged in her own home, trapped in her own life and continually bursting out in anger or boiling within herself. And I thought of her son who had been the victim of her own frustration. Situations like hers are tragic and contribute to much waste in life, and the waste of people and emotions always saddens me. Also, I wondered about her husband. Was he like many of the other Swedish men I had met? I remembered that about two hours ago at the party, I had asked a Swedish trade union leader what was his opinion of the Schuman Plan and what did he think about criticisms of the Plan which had but recently been made by the British Labor Party.

"That is not a Swedish question," he had answered me.

I told myself:

—This woman, Helga Svenson, is not merely a Swedish question.

"I couldn't stay at home and do nothing," she repeated in a tone of challenge.

The other men picked up her remark and the conversation turned into a discussion of the role of women in society. I suddenly asked her: "What do you think of *Hedda Gabler?*"

Helga turned quickly toward me and said in a quick rush of enthusiasm: "She was right. She was right. She was right to leave her home."

"That wasn't Hedda," I said. "That was Nora in *A Doll's House*. What do you think of Hedda?"

"I don't know it. I never heard of her. I don't know anything about her," she said, her voice dull. She turned away from me evasively.

"You must know—you must have read or seen Ibsen's *Hedda Gabler,*" I said.

"I never heard of her," she said weakly.

"Men are doing it to us. They are making us wretched," she said vehemently a few moments later.

"What are they doing?" one of the trade unionists asked.

"They don't treat us as equals."

"But we are trying to do that in America," Oliver said. "That's one of the things my union has fought for."

She ignored his remark. And her voice grew thick with an anger that was full of hatred as she said: "But we will get our revenge. They will treat us better or we will destroy their sons. . . . *We will destroy their sons.*"

"Why do you say that?" I asked.

She stared at me, perplexed, as though my question were utterly beyond comprehension.

"In Europe," Oliver said, "women aren't as free as in America. In France . . ."

"At least in France," she interrupted, "they are treated like women. But if they don't change, we will have our revenge."

"If you had it in your power to create the most ideal, the best possible conditions in the world for women, what would you do?" I asked her.

Her eyes turned on me and grew bright as she answered me: "I'd make the men do everything that we do. I'd make them do all the drudgery that we have to." She paused. Then with her voice throbbing, she added, speaking slowly and with careful enunciation: "Science proves that one sex is not necessary. And it isn't woman."

She stared at us, one by one, in defiance.

We continued talking, but when Helga had said, with concentrated passion, that men were not necessary in the world, a climax had been reached. It seemed to me that with this assertion, she had said all that she wished or wanted to say. Never in her life had she had an experience such as this one with us; it gave her an opportunity to talk to men on a level of frankness and equality and to tell them all that she thought of and resented in them. She would not have spoken in the same manner to a group of Swedish men, and she probably would not even have dared to. And having had a good time vituperating men to their faces, she quickly relaxed. The sullen defiance went out of her. She sank back on the sofa and spoke flatly, dully.

But by this time, everyone had done enough talking, and we were hungry. The conversation had reached a dramatic high point, and what was then said was anti-climatic and repetitive. There was a silent moment. Then Helga became suddenly feminine and flirtatious. She smiled like a woman. Her eyes shone softly. She looked meekly at me and then similarly at the others.

The neat young maid announced that dinner was ready and we all sat at the big table in the next room. As we began eating, our conversation turned away from Helga and onto questions of Swedish economy in which we were interested and which we had discussed before. We had speculated about the possibility of Sweden producing washing machines in quantity for sale and the domestic consumption. Washing machines and also other items of labor-saving household machines were spoken of by Swedish women and, in fact, Helga had expressed envy of American women because so many of them have these machines. We speculated further about washing machines, but Helga was very quiet and did not join in our discussion. Was it economically possible for Sweden to manufacture washing machines in quantity for her domestic market? Would these be purchased? Did Sweden have a sufficient machine-tool industry to permit this and also to produce other commodities for an internal consumer market? I might add that this conversation can suggest something that had been happening all over Europe. At dinner parties, cocktail parties and on other occasions where Europeans and Americans meet, conversation often turns on questions of production, markets and economy of European countries. This was a feature of life of the new or changing Europe of the Cold War.

While we were continuing our discussion, our host, Ray, asked the maid if she had oil paintings in her home. In all Swedish homes oil paintings are hung. She answered "Yes." Then he asked if she had a washing machine, and her answer was "No." Which did she prefer? A washing machine, but she quickly added that she never expected to be able to have one.

We continued eating and talking, and more or less agreed that in Sweden and also in other European countries outside of the Iron Curtain, an appeal along the lines of the New Deal would be received with enthusiasm provided that political and economic circumstances would make this appeal practical and possible. And as we went on talking and eating, there was Helga. Now she smiled easier and her eyes were brighter. Her sullenness was gone. She was a different kind of woman with six men than she had been shortly before. She was flirtatious. But even so, now and then gloom would stretch across her face. She would sink away into withdrawn moments. And noticing her, I kept wondering. Where were we all going? Paradise is not gained with machinery. Social improvement, for which we had and were continuing to struggle, will not solve and ease all the problems of the souls of men—and of women. There are other things besides comfort and convenience in this world. There are hungers and angers of the human spirit. And as a fresh new smile came on her face, I told myself that probably these hungers and angers would never be satisfied and appeased. Perhaps they reflect incurable conditions in the human soul. There is love and war in every one of us, and had not Helga exploded under the pressure of the love and war that was within her? Yes, there she was, attractive and appealing, almost beautiful, and she was at war with herself. She was all of these problems which we had been discussing, and she was flesh and blood like us, too. She was suffering flesh and blood.

After dinner, she shook hands with all of us and thanked us graciously for the conversation. She smiled and made eyes at us, invited us to come to her home and to sit and have a drink in her garden. She repeated the invitation and reiterated that she had enjoyed herself very much. And as she said still one more goodbye, I saw both meekness and apology in those dark, changing eyes of hers.

I watched her walk to the front door. Her gait was slow and spiritless. I've never seen her again.

Little Johnny: *A Fable*

Little Johnny was not a bad boy; he was only misunderstood. A legion of social workers, psychiatric social workers, psychiatrists, reformers, and sundry other professional and amateur understanders of misunderstood little boys—all of them had a hand in understanding misunderstood Little Johnny. And all and sundry came to the one same conclusion: Little Johnny needed to be understood.

The career of Little Johnny began on a street where poor people lived. He was a beautiful little boy who looked very much like an angel. One fine day, he was playing with youngsters his own age. The girls were playing hopscotch, and Little Johnny suddenly gave one of the girls a shove. She fell down a cellar stairway and landed on her head; her skull was cracked. In the ensuing melee and excitement, Little Johnny withdrew to the edge of the crowd and gazed on the scene with wide-eyed and angelic innocence shining on his face. A kindly old lady noticed him and exclaimed.

"What a beautiful little boy."

Just then the ambulance drew up for the girl with the shattered skull, and something happened to Little Johnny's cathexes: they got tangled up. He noticed a large pane of window glass standing beside an iron picket fence. Grabbing it, he smashed the glass on the head of a playmate and thus a little boy was also carried off to the hospital, along with the little girl who had been playing hopscotch.

Little Johnny was carefully investigated for the first time. The result of the investigation revealed that he was the son of a poor man, that he was hungry, and that he was misunderstood. These facts had sparked off his aggressions, and it was decided and resolved that food and understanding would put his cathexes back into place. Then he would be able to control his hostility and become adjusted.

The first task, then, in socializing the aggressions of Little Johnny was that of providing him with more vitamins and calories. This was quickly arranged. The next afternoon a grocery boy was dispatched to the dreary flat where Little Johnny was housed in misunderstanding with his underprivileged parents. Little Johnny was at home. His aggressions had produced two funerals, and there was a pall upon the street. He had no one to play with, and he was lonesome.

The grocery boy came puffing up the narrow stairway, lugging a big box of food. This gave promise of winning Little Johnny's confidence, and then he would soon be launched on the calm seas of understanding and a happy boyhood.

But Little Johnny was lonesome. He had no one to play with on that particular afternoon. So the grocery boy was more than welcome and Little Johnny was glad to see him. But the grocery boy was busy. He had to hurry back to the store where he worked in order to deliver more boxes of groceries. And since Little Johnny was lonesome and had no one to play with, he became a misunderstood little boy, and his aggressions erupted into a volcanic act of misunderstanding. This action took the symptomatic form of Little Johnny grabbing a milk bottle from the box of groceries and conking the grocery boy on the skull.

The grocery boy was stretched out on the floor of the mean kitchen in Little Johnny's poor home.

Little Johnny was further investigated and studied while the grocery boy was laid away to his eternal rest.

The new study and investigation scientifically confirmed the conclusions of the original one. There was now no doubt but that Little Johnny was misunderstood. A new plan was launched to bring understanding to Little Johnny so that his aggressions could, as the saying went, be socialized.

He didn't have a clean home. He needed one. A

housing project was gotten under way, and it was explained to Little Johnny that he was a good boy, not a bad boy, and that when he lived in the brand-new home in the brand-new building that was being constructed, he would be an even better boy.

Time elapsed and Little Johnny's aggressions subsided somewhat. He tied a tin can to the tail of a dog, threw a rock at an alley cat and made some sport with flies and bedbugs, but there were no more funerals in the neighborhood.

In due time, and thanks to modern engineering efficiency, a beautiful new building sprang up and Little Johnny was housed in a shiny, brand-new home. An article was written in a technical journal on Little Johnny's case and it proved that understanding conquered the aggressions which were unleashed from the unconscious of a little boy who was not at all bad—but only misunderstood.

The three funerals were forgotten and Little Johnny became a hero of his neighborhood. For, as a result of his aggressions, there stood this impressive new building where many other families besides his own could live in comfort.

The case of Little Johnny appeared to be closed. The records were ready to be filed away. His aggressions were now put to peaceful sleep in his little unconscious. Two more articles on his case appeared in technical journals.

But then, suddenly, there was a new uproar in Little Johnny's unconscious and before this uproar could be understood, Little Johnny sprang out of bed in the dead of night, stubbed his toe, scurried to the kitchen, and found a butcher knife.

The use he made of this symbolic instrument resulted in the funeral of his father two days later.

The situation then became serious indeed. Somewhere along the line of therapy and understanding, something had gone wrong, and this had detached some violently strong sector of Little Johnny's id. But still, for a period, Little Johnny had been good and had not even molested a tomcat.

A new investigation was initiated. So Little Johnny was studied and investigated once again and by new investigators who had the proper training and were fully qualified to understand that violent and detached sector of poor Little Johnny's id.

Little Johnny now had a good clean home and good food, and this had kept the angel quiet until the fateful night when he had dispatched his father to the better world. This proved that the attack on Little Johnny's id had been sound if not a total success.

How was Little Johnny now misunderstood? That was the question. It was studied carefully, and so was Little Johnny. Fresh study revealed that Little Johnny did not have a place where he could play like a happy and normal boy whose aggressions could be taken out in play that would have no connection with the mortality statistics.

This also was clearly and fully explained to Little Johnny and he was told that he was still a good boy and that he need have no fear because he would be given a place where he could play.

And this is how a playground came to be built in Little Johnny's neighborhood.

Little Johnny romped and played and laughed in the playground, and more illuminating papers on Little Johnny were written in technical journals. These were read and studied far and wide in colleges and among the people whose profession it is to understand where there is often neither light nor understanding.

The father's bones were at peaceful rest, but his spirit looked down on Little Johnny, blissful with the knowledge that his little boy was now happy and understood.

Time elapsed. Little Johnny was growing. His cheeks were red and healthy, and he was daily enriched with vitamins. Every afternoon when school let out and all day on Saturday, he and the other youngsters ran and romped in the new playground. They enjoyed healthy fun.

And then, one Saturday in the springtime, Little Johnny happened to have a baseball bat in his hand. Something again went wrong in the id of Little Johnny. The head of the director of the new playground was round, and so was a baseball. Little Johnny's symbols became intermixed. He swung the bat like a true—if miniature—Joe

DiMaggio, and the director soon received a harp and became an accompanist to a choir of angels.

After the funeral of the director, a new and more serious attack was made on the problem of Little Johnny's aggressions. After all the previous studies and efforts to understand him, his id was still a bit riotous and he was continuing to live in clouds of misunderstanding. Something was wrong. Some aspect of his nature had gone unapprehended. With all the time, the care, the study, the understanding that had gone into his case, he still retained some of his little aggressions in an unsocialized form. What was being misunderstood? For Little Johnny was not at all a bad boy. He had good marks in school and he played well except in these sudden moments when he blew up because he was misunderstood and his hostilities became linked up with those symbols which unfortunately produced an increase in the income of the local mortician.

So the areas of misunderstanding in Little Johnny were further probed and new experts were brought into the case.

One of the new experts had only recently written a profound and revolutionary book entitled *Aggressions and Aesthetics,* and this book gave the clue to understanding those free-floating fragments of Little Johnny's id.

Briefly, it was discovered that bread and a home and a playground were not enough to bring light into the dark unconscious of little boys like Little Johnny. What Little Johnny needed was beauty. In order to provide Little Johnny with the opportunity to grow up and become a good man, it was necessary that he be allowed "to play amid things of beauty" as Plato foresaw in his *Republic.*

And this is how a beautiful park was created in Little Johnny's neighborhood. Little Johnny loved the flowers. He loved to smell the roses. He rolled on the grass. He climbed the trees. He breathed the air of nature. He was happy and most well-behaved. But one Saturday afternoon in the springtime, Little Johnny was smelling the aroma of the beautiful roses and by chance he noticed a pair of shears which a gardener had left lying beside a rose bed.

The gardener was kneeling down at work a few feet away, and he didn't see Little Johnny.

Now the gardener is no more, and a further study is being made of Little Johnny's aggressions. But in the meantime, the effort to understand these aggressions has resulted in the reconstruction of Little Johnny's old neighborhood. It has become a model of improvements. And perhaps the affair of the gardener, the shears, and the rosebushes will lead to new improvements and to a final insight into the mystery of Little Johnny's misunderstood id.

The latest report on the case is that the investigators are still probing in order to apprehend the symbolic meaning of shears and roses in poor Little Johnny's psyche. But inasmuch as they have unraveled the meaning of hopscotch, panes of glass, milk bottles, butcher knives, and baseball bats, they are not totally in the dark. They have learned much about the boy's psyche already. His case is fully documented, and the investigators are confident that they will soon learn what shears mean to him. Once they do, more progress can be made in the case. There remains solid and substantial reason to believe that Little Johnny will be understood, rather than misunderstood, and all of the neighbors hope that a beach or a swimming pool will be created to help understand Little Johnny and to socialize his aggressions, because if this is done, then Little Johnny will have produced the model neighborhood of America.

Boys and Girls

Iris sat listening to the guys tell dirty stories. She looked innocent, and her face was a small and pretty oval incarnating purity and virginity. She told some good stories herself, and the guys laughed raucously. She always got excited thinking of boys, because she knew she had a power over them, and that she could get them all pop-eyed any time she wanted to. And she liked to sit as she was now, tantalizing them, having them look at her a long time, before she let them start the fireworks. She thought that this was a very funny thing to do, and it made her feel very important.

She rose and circled the room, walking as she imagined Theda Bara would if Theda Bara were in a room full of heroes. She kept telling them not to get sore eyes, because she didn't like to be the cause of anybody becoming a four-eyes. She stopped before Mush Joss and told him that she wasn't poison ivory. Then she sat down again on the flower-designed rug and told Red to tell them all some more dirty jokes. Red said that she was a dirty enough joke, and they laughed, and then he told some jokes. She sang "Rings on My Fingers" and "My Lulu." She told Jerry Rooney and Hugh Nolan, one of Jim Nolan's younger brothers, that they were both pretty young and they would have to be careful not to get cross-eyed. She sat sighing and thinking that she would start the parade soon. She felt good and thought that it was awful nice for boys and girls to play with each other.

Studs sat pop-eyed like the rest of the bunch. He talked as if all this were ordinary, and he knew what doing it was like. He sat looking holes through Iris, excited, afraid. After a pun of Red's, Jerry rolled on the floor, laughing like he had the St. Vitus's dance, and the guys kidded him about being a punk. They were going to take his britches off, but Iris wouldn't have it. She took Jerry into her mother's bedroom and told the guys to shake dice for their turns. As the door closed on them, Red said: "And a little child will lead them."

Everybody laughed. As they shook dice for turns, there was a lot of rough stuff and kidding. Studs won first crack.

He sat while Red told another dirty joke. At last he would do it. He told himself that this was luck. But he was afraid and upset. He remembered once in the eighth grade during Holy Week, Sister Battling Bertha had said that it was the sins of the flesh that God used as a test to see whether or not you were worthy of going to Heaven. Studs wondered, and he suddenly thought that he was paying too little attention to religion and his soul. Sometimes, after he committed a sin, he was afraid of death, and now he feared he had already committed a mortal sin by wanting to do it with Iris and listening to jokes, and he was about to commit an even more grievous mortal sin. He was awfully afraid, all right, and he guessed he must be a sinful guy or something. His conscience told him it was not right, but there he was, wanting to do it anyway. And how could he back out? Maybe he'd be good and careful the next time and not let himself get into the occasion of sin. But how could Studs Lonigan show a yellow streak now? If he did, he'd make himself into a laughingstock, with everybody giving him the merry ha-ha. And that was no way for a tough guy to act. Not by a damn sight. And he was losing his breath, just like he was yellow and trying to sneak out of a fight.

He had to go through with it, but still he wished he had made some excuse before coming up. He wished he were somewhere else. He determined he would be different in the future. He would receive the sacraments and pray regularly, and be forgiven, and try to win grace enough so that he could lead a better life. He would go to confession next Saturday night, and he'd try to be really and truly sorry for his sins. He promised Our Lord and the Blessed Virgin that he would never do it again. He found himself suddenly imagining what Hell was like, and it

made him sweat with fear. It was hotter than a Gary
steel mill, and there were all the souls in it, burning in
fires, their suffering faces looking worse than if they had
been mashed by a motor truck. And then he laughed and
forgot about Hell because of a joke Red told them.

He talked with the guys to get his conscience off his
mind, and he told them that it would be *Ummmmm* and
sweet, and that if that punk Jerry didn't hurry up, he'd
be losing some buttons. He talked and suddenly, for no
reason at all, death seemed to walk through him like a
skeleton, and he got awfully afraid again, and he wished
that he wasn't there.

He knew he was starting to lose his nerve and getting
leery about the idea of it, and the idea of letting a girl see
him. He talked so they wouldn't suspect how he felt, and
he wished it was over and it was tomorrow and he was
somewhere else. He wondered too how he could stall and
get some other guy to go in first. He wondered what
would happen if her old lady came home. He thought of
Lucy, Lucy sitting in a tree, swinging her legs, the wind
on them both, and she seemed to him cool like that wind,
and he was all hot and miserable, and he wished that he
were cool and with Lucy. She'd hate him if she should ever
find out, and he'd never be able to make it up with her

Jerry came out, his face coloring, and Iris told them he
wasn't very much of a man, and they kidded him, telling
him to get strong on egg malted milks and to grow hair
on his chest. Paulie Haggerty got Iris by him and tried to
grab her, but she walked away. He crabbed so that Weary
Reilly told him not to be a dynamiter. Red told her to
get back to business.

"Who's first?" she asked.

Studs got red, but he didn't try to get out of it. He
couldn't talk, so he just got up and walked to the door,
feeling like a condemned man.

Studs came out disappointed, sunk. It wasn't so much.
It was nothing like he thought it would be. And it all
ended in a bigger hurry than he thought it would. It
wasn't any more fun than lots of things. He told them that
she was waiting for the next guy. They asked him how it

was, and he said it was *Ummmmmm*. He said it because that was the way it was supposed to be.

Davey Cohen went in and found Iris lying on the bed. When he entered, she insisted that she wouldn't let him touch her. He got hot and very sore, but she didn't care. She called him bowlegged, and he called her a bitch. He stood trying to think of worse things to call her, and he was as hot as a steam roller. She told him to get out. If he didn't, she would get Weary Reilly and the guys to sock him, and they would, because if they didn't, she would call off the party.

"You goddamn bitch, I ought to sock your teeth!" he said.

"Runt! Jus' try it! Jus' try it! Jus' try it, that's all! Jus' try it!"

He left the room. When the guys asked him what was wrong, he didn't answer and walked out of the apartment. Iris came out, proud, saying she didn't like him, and Weary agreed with her.

"Next?" she asked.

Paulie Haggerty was Johnny-on-the-spot and as flushed as a beet. She told him to hurry because she had a day's work ahead of her.

"No need to hurry. I can keep you busy for a long time, a long time," Paulie leered.

They told him not to get caught trying it. Studs told Paulie he wasn't such a good working man as he thought, and they laughed.

"Paulie, don't do nothing I wouldn't do," Red called at him.

"Leave it to your Uncle Dudley. *Ummmmm!*" Paulie exclaimed, following Iris out of the parlor.

Waiting, they gassed and shot craps for pennies. Weary was impatient and kept wanting them all to get a move on. He and Tommy Doyle talked tough to each other, and the guys hoped a fight would start, but they were disappointed. Mush Joss won a nickel and boasted that it was his first crap game.

"How was it, Studs?" asked Jerry.

"*Ummmmmmmmmmm!*" Studs exclaimed.

They boasted about what they would do, and bragged

of what they had already done with girls. Hugh Nolan
tried to talk of his experiences, but they told him to shut
up because he was only a punk. One by one they went in
and came out, *Ummmmmmm*ing. The guys who had had
their turns kept urging the others, so that there could be
a second round. Hugh Nolan was next to last. When his
turn came, Weary couldn't wait any longer and went in.
Hugh crabbed, but Weary told him to shut up. Hugh did.

They waited while Weary was in there, hoping that they
could get in again. But Weary never seemed to come out,
and nobody wanted to bang on the door, because Weary
was tough. Even Studs, who had licked him, didn't want
to interrupt.

After the gang shag, Iris would have Weary up every
time she could because she said Weary was nicer than
anybody else. So Weary would go up to see her. Until
one day, while he was there, the bell rang. He didn't hear
it. The bell rang again. Iris's mother found her key in her
pocketbook and entered. She was fat and middle-aged, a
lump of indistinguishable female flesh. Moving around,
she found her daughter in bed with Weary. She screamed
and fell into a mock faint. The faint was a failure. If
she remained down on the floor, the villain might escape.
She got to her feet while Weary was quickly dressing.

"You cur!" the mother screamed in a high-pitched
voice.

Weary scowled.

"Who are you? What's your name? What right have
you in my house? Ruining my daughter! My poor innocent little girl. What'll her father say? I'll put you in the
reform school. If her father caught you, he'd kill you.
Killing is too good for a dirty little sonofabitch like you.
You little cur! My God! My little girl! Ruined! Disgraced!
What'll the neighbors say? You ruined Iris. You pig! And
you, you, Iris, you filthy little whore! You're no daughter
of mine! Did he make you do it? The cur! You whore!
Help! Oh God! God! I'll call the police and put you behind bars. My poor little girl!"

Iris hid her head under the sheets and cried like a
small, frightened child.

"What's your name?" the mother demanded of Weary.

"None of your goddamn business."

"You cur! I'll put you behind bars. I'll put you in the reform school! I'll have you hung! Tell me your name! Dog! Beast!"

Iris peered out from the sheets and, red-eyed, she begged her mother to stop.

"Shut up, you slut!" her mother cried. She clutched Weary, shook him, and spat in his face. "Tell me your name!"

"Take your hands off me, you old bitch!" Weary sullenly commanded.

His command quelled the mother. He started to leave. She told him to stop. He turned to stick his tongue out at her. He leered, thumbed his nose. She asked Iris who he was, but the girl refused to answer. She cried tragically. Weary left. The mother fainted.

Weary walked out the front entrance and lit a cigarette. He met the guys from the gang at Fifty-eighth and Prairie. Davey was around trying to explain how he didn't care about what Iris had done to him that time, and, anyway, he was blowing town and going on the bum. Weary interrupted him and told them what had happened at Iris's. They nearly laughed their guts out, it was so funny. And they admired Weary. It was damn funny. Only now they wouldn't be able to go up there any more. Red said, what if they couldn't? The world was full of young bitches like Iris.

Edna's Husband

My wife Minnie and I used to see them sometimes at the Café du Dôme or among the crowds on the sidewalks of the Boulevard Montparnasse at night. I noticed Jeremiah and Edna before I met them, and I could tell they were Americans. They seemed utterly lost and out of place. Edna was tall, and Jeremiah was short. She was drab and looked ageless. The mere sight of her, with her shabby black dress, her cotton stockings, her homely face, her dejected expression, her thin, straight hair the color of dishwater, was enough to sink my spirits. Jeremiah had an obtuse, stupid, and freckled face. His ears were so big that they gave him a very comical appearance. His trousers were too short, and his suit coat always fit him too tightly. Sometimes at night, they would walk slowly up one side of the Boulevard Montparnasse and down the other, rarely talking to each other, and scarcely even looking at anyone else. Edna's posture was ungainly, and she hunched her shoulders. Jeremiah held his head rigidly. Back and forth they would stroll, and I wondered what thoughts were simmering in their minds.

I lived in a big new building in Montrouge where I had a large studio room with a north light. I'm a painter. I'd noticed Jeremiah and Edna before I knew they lived in my building, and I saw them on the stairs several times before they'd talk to me, and then, after that, it took a few more weeks before we got farther than saying hello. But once that point was reached, they called on us often to borrow something or other. I came to know more about them than anyone else in the dwindling colony of Montparnasse Americans.

They came from the Deep South. Jeremiah called him-

31

self an artist. I saw some of his canvases. He had no talent, and his pictures aren't really worth discussing. He had won a prize fellowship with a stipend of twenty-four hundred dollars in a competition sponsored by the Springer Yeast Company. How yeast and art got mixed up is something I never understood. It was probably a public relations or advertising stunt of some sort. Why Jeremiah won this contest is also beyond me. I remember some of us used to laugh over this in the Dôme or the Select, and I once remarked I wouldn't want to see the work of those who had lost to Jeremiah in the contest. I call him by his name here, but actually we all came to refer to him as "Edna's husband."

He and Edna arrived in Paris in May, 1931. He never showed his pictures to anyone except me. He rarely talked about painting; in fact, he rarely talked. When he did say something, it was in a slow, drawling voice. In his presence, Edna was always cowed and silent. If she tried to speak, one look from him was sufficient to silence her.

They had no friends in Paris, unless you'd call Minnie and me their friends. They always addressed us as Mr. and Mrs. Levin. As I said, they liked to borrow from us, and Jeremiah was pleased whenever we'd feed Edna for him.

They weren't long in the Montparnasse circles before they were ticketed as spongers. Almost every day they would hang around the offices of the American Express Company on the Rue Scribe, looking as lost and as out of place as they did on the Boulevard Montparnasse. They would try to strike up a conversation with an unsuspecting American tourist. Edna would do most of the talking. She would explain that they were poor Americans, that her husband was an artist, and that they scarcely had enough to eat. In this way they sometimes even managed to find a sucker who took them to an expensive restaurant.

Whenever Jeremiah did talk, it was usually about food. He would ask questions about restaurants and food prices in restaurants. Several times I saw them sitting in a café, studying a map of Paris. He and Edna could use their knowledge of restaurants, food prices and streets with the sympathetic American tourists they picked up.

Sometimes Edna went out alone, wearing her most ragged black dress. She always carried a large, worn black leather pocketbook. She used to put dried beans in it, and she would take these out and hold them in the palm of her calloused and sweaty hand and mournfully explain that these were what Jeremiah made her eat. She would tell people that she was always hungry, if not half-starved. Whenever she got a free meal from us or induced someone to buy her a dinner, she wolfed her food like a starved animal. It was unpleasant to see her eat. Also, she'd tell us all she had to wear rags because Jeremiah wouldn't allow her to buy a decent dress. Several women gave her old clothes, but she still managed to look as poor and ragged and dejected as she did in her black dresses. Bemoaning her fate, Edna also complained of Jeremiah's cruelty and selfishness. By himself, she claimed, he would eat well, with an appetite that could never be satisfied, and she couldn't, for the life of her, understand why he wasn't fat. And he would lock up food so she couldn't have it, and he would force her out of the house so he could eat to his heart's content. She repeated these stories until everyone was bored with them. One day after we had heard her tell them for the sixth or seventh time, Minnie asked her why she didn't leave a man as piggish and selfish as Jeremiah.

"Oh, I couldn't do that," Edna answered, bursting into tears.

Moved by this, we fed her, but I had to leave the table. I couldn't watch her eat that night.

There isn't much more to say of Jeremiah and Edna. There was no surprise in them. They behaved just as I've described them, and this became a matter of endless repetition. Minnie and I had to avoid them because they bored us and sponged on us too much. I was only a poor artist without a scholarship, fellowship, or even a free cake of yeast!

One day in the summer, however, after we had successfully avoided them for about three weeks, there was a knock on our door. It was Jeremiah. He entered our apartment before Minnie asked him in, and we could see that something was troubling him. He was quite pale. He stood in the center of the living room for about two minutes, saying nothing, and swallowing hard so that his Adam's apple moved noticeably.

"Jeremiah, is anything the matter?" Minnie asked.

Jeremiah answered after a long pause:

"I was thinking . . ."

Minnie and I waited to hear what he was thinking about. He looked like a frightened rabbit.

"What's the matter? What are you thinking about, Jeremiah?" Minnie asked.

"Ah . . ." he paused. "Ah, can you come downstairs and get the glass out of Edna?"

Minnie and I were bewildered and flabbergasted. We didn't know what Jeremiah was talking about. Then Minnie guessed what he meant.

"But what is it, Jeremiah?" she asked.

"Yes . . . can you help me get the glass out of Edna?" Jeremiah asked, speaking in his slow, drawling voice.

We went downstairs to his apartment. It was a filthy mess. It probably hadn't been swept in two weeks and there was stale food on the table. But Jeremiah was unperturbed.

We found Edna lying on an unmade bed, bleeding.

"She has to go to the hospital," Minnie said, alarmed.

"Yes?" Jeremiah asked dumbly.

He stood in the center of the room, casual in his manner, acting as though nothing was wrong with his wife.

Minnie argued with Jeremiah for about fifteen minutes, trying to convince him of the urgency of taking Edna to the American Hospital. But Jeremiah was not easily convinced. He explained that he had been given this "glass contrivance" in Mississippi, and that he had been told that it would prevent babies. There was a bulb on the end of it and this had broken inside Edna.

Edna was pale, too frightened now to cry out. She lay there, silent, gazing at us with the same begging expression in her eyes that she had when she would ask strangers to buy her a meal. I was embarrassed and didn't look at her.

Jeremiah finally yielded to Minnie's arguments. But he didn't think that he needed to take a cab.

"You take her in a taxicab right this minute. Go ahead!" Minnie said so commandingly that he trembled.

Jeremiah obeyed. He went out to find a taxicab, returned, and we helped Edna downstairs to the waiting cab.

The glass was extracted from Edna. She survived and continued to haunt Montparnasse and the American Express Company, looking drab and ageless, begging for meals and complaining of the way that Jeremiah treated her. After about three months Jeremiah left her. He ran off with an alcoholic Englishwoman. We did what we could feed Edna, but we couldn't afford much. She was sent back to America by charity. I never heard what happened afterward to Edna or her husband, but they were just about the weirdest Americans in Montparnasse back in the days when we lived there. And that's saying something, because I met some first-class weirdies.

I've often told this story and laughed, and others have laughed when they heard it. But there never is any real mirth in my laughter. It's bitter laughter. Such human ignorance, stupidity, backwardness pains me. It always has. And I always wondered how and for what Edna's husband won that scholarship in art from a yeast company.

A Saturday Night in America

Teresa lived with her sister-in-law in two small rooms on the top floor of an enormous old mansion on upper Fifth Avenue. The building was going to ruin, and some of the floors were not rented. Teresa was thirty years old, blond and round and pretty. Her hair was thick and her eyes were blue. Her face was full and oval. She had a good figure. What few clothes she had fitted her well, and when she walked along the streets of New York she could easily have passed for an American girl whose experiences might have been more or less like those of thousands of other American girls.

But eight years before, Teresa had been in a slave camp in the Soviet Arctic. When the Red Army invaded Poland, she had been a law student in a Polish university. She was picked up by the Russians, and when they interrogated her, the fact that she spoke Russian aroused their suspicion. Teresa had studied Russian in school. She was arrested, herded into a freight car with many others and taken by stages to a slave camp in the Arctic. She spent more than a year in the camp. What she had to say of her experiences there corresponded with the accounts thousands have now given. She spoke of the cruelty of the guards, of the neglect of the prisoners, of the brutally hard work which was often beyond their strength, of how hunger and starvation were used as a spur to increased labor, of suffering from the bitter cold with inadequate clothing, of other prisoners dying, of families broken up, perhaps forever. Also, she spoke of how there was not even the most elementary provision for feminine hygiene in the slave camp.

Teresa had not only survived, but she had managed to

36

conduct herself so that she had not been violated or seduced by any of the guards. At the time of the Sikorski agreement she was released and, along with another Polish girl, she made her way to Moscow. There she got herself shipped to the south where she joined the Polish Army. She left the territory of the Soviet Union through Persia, got to Egypt by hitchhiking an airplane ride, and served in a division of Polish volunteers. She was discharged because of the headaches and earaches which were a consequence of her stay in the Arctic prison camp. She hitchhiked an airplane ride from Cairo to London and during the remainder of the war, did clerical work for the Polish Government-in-Exile in London.

Before the war, Teresa had always imagined that someday she would have a chance to visit the United States. As a girl and young student in Poland, she had often dreamed of making this journey. But this had then been something far-off, a dream she wanted one day to come true. Her family was middle-class, and as a student she had been nonpolitical. She had never imagined that politics would lead to her coming to America. But world politics and the war had brought her to London by way of the Soviet Arctic, Moscow, Soviet Asia, Persia and Egypt. Why couldn't she go on to America? After the war she went to the American Consulate and asked for a visa. Naturally, she was closely interrogated. Why should she want to go to America? she was asked. She could only answer simply that she wanted to go. She told the Vice-Consul that she had no reason at all except that she yearned to go to America, that before the war she had wanted to go, and that she had always imagined that in some way or other she would get there. Teresa was given a visa.

Now Teresa was a stateless person. Her visa had expired, and she was regularly visited by immigration officials concerning her status. They were sympathetic, and she had no trouble with her papers other than the slight annoyance of periodic interviews.

Her sister-in-law, Julia, had gotten to America from Germany after the war. Julia's husband, a seaman, gave the two young women a hundred and twenty-five dollars a month, on which they lived.

Teresa was bright and friendly. She seemed to wear lightly the burden of her experiences in the slave camp. She talked of them readily and often, as did many of the Poles who came to America in the first postwar years. She was an energetic young woman. She had not been in America long before she had managed to get into contact with the editor of a mass-circulation magazine; she told him of an article she wanted to write, describing her experiences in the Soviet camp. Now she was writing a book on life in the camp in which she had been enslaved.

Teresa had a name-day party one chilly spring Saturday night. She and Julia had scarcely enough money on which to live. For weeks they had saved out of their budget, and they knew that for some weeks afterward, unless they were the unexpected beneficiaries of fortune, they would have to live very frugally. But they had piled the top of an old chest of drawers with all kinds of food—fruits, nuts, sandwiches, and cakes. Also they had bought wine and brandy.

All but two of their twelve guests were Polish. These two were American men interested in fighting slave labor. Of the other ten, every one was a postwar immigrant to America and every one had been in one or another concentration camp in Europe. They sat in chairs, on the sofa and on the floor, talking. The atmosphere was gay and pleasant. Teresa and Julia kept serving food and drinks, offering one platter after another. Everyone ate heartily and continually. Then they sang Polish songs, some plaintive, others joyful. The two Americans listened, but they were mere spectators and were pretty much out of the swing of the evening. They had no common memories with these Poles. The songs involved another world, a world far away and gone forever from the lives of Teresa and her friends, except as this world lingered in the songs they were singing, in the language they talked among themselves and in their memories.

Teresa had had no news of her mother for several years. She did not even know if her mother were living or dead. With every Pole in the room it was similar. Some loved one, some relative, was unheard of, unaccounted for. They were all here in this foreign land, speaking a language that was not their native tongue, looking at streets and buildings that formed the background and the stage props of the memories and the past of others, of Americans. They were not Americans, but only Americans-to-be. Three, four, five or more years had been stolen from their lives. Out of childhood and adolescence they had emerged—or they had been emerging—into young manhood and young womanhood when the war had come. Foreign soldiers and a foreign police had snatched them off. And now they were living on this new continent, making new lives for themselves.

As they sang, all joining in, the past welled up for them, and they were again outside of America, away from the foreign world in which they were making their adjustments. They were back in the homes of their childhood, back in the time before they became victims of history, forcibly thrust out into a world of slavery and terror and cruelty and human bestiality. They were asserting and affirming their own past with these songs of love and death, of joy and sorrow, songs which were so much a part of the culture they had lost. They were able to do in mind what they would possibly never be able to do again in fact—they were walking again the streets of the villages and towns and cities of their childhood.

They sang for almost an hour. And as they sang and talked and ate and drank, they became increasingly more spirited. Teresa seemed to grow in attractiveness as the evening wore on. She spoke and sang, sometimes with joy, sometimes with sadness. It was apparent that she truly enjoyed her name-day party.

After much singing and talking, a quiet suddenly came over them. Conversation became random. The spirit, the elation, had gone out of the party. It was about eleven o'clock, too early to break up, especially since it was a Saturday night.

A big lean man in his early thirties began speaking. He was an engineer. He talked of a German concentration camp. When he had been kept there, during the war, he never could have imagined how one day he would be free in America. Yet he had always gone on believing that one day he'd again be free. Teresa said that she had thought the same way. But, she added, she had had no reason whatever for thinking and hoping to escape or be liberated. She believed that she had retained her hope because she was Polish. Yet nothing could have been worse than being in the camp where she had been in the Arctic.

Julia interrupted to say that her camp in Germany had been worse. They all began talking at once, debating which of the concentration camps, the Nazi or the Soviet, had been the worst. Those who had been in the Soviet camps—and there were more of them present—insisted it had been the Russian ones. Those, like Julia, who had been inmates of the German camps, seemed to stand on a point of pride and insisted that they had had an infinitely worse time.

They compared their conditions of slavery, describing the cruelties they had seen or been the victim of; starvation, suffering, disease, degradation. They put into words, however, only a small fraction of the horrors they had witnessed and experienced. To the two Americans, all of this seemed completely remote, impossibly far away from the two rooms at the top of the disintegrating, run-down old brownstone mansion on upper Fifth Avenue. It even seemed somewhat unreal to the Poles themselves. They might have been describing and talking about what they had experienced in nightmares, instead of in waking life.

The discussion of concentration camps went on for some time. Julia in particular insisted that the German camps had been the worst; as a point of principle she maintained her position. When she was reminded that she had not been in the Russian camps, she replied that some of the others had not been in the German camps.

The engineer interrupted, declaring that he had been in both German and Russian camps and that he'd thought often of the conditions in both. If he had to choose, he said, he'd prefer to go to a German rather than a Soviet camp. His remarks settled the discussion. Talk became apathetic, and soon the guests started to leave.

When they had all gone, Teresa spoke with her sister-in-law for a few minutes, both of them happy and excited.

Then they washed the dishes and put the food away and straightened up their rooms. With this done, Julia went to bed. Teresa didn't want to sleep. She didn't know what she wanted to do. She was very restless. Memories of girlhood flooded upon her. She felt a profound yearning, a deep longing for the days of her childhood.

She went to the window and looked out at Central Park in the midnight darkness. She could hear the wind in the trees, and she could hear the wind against the window. The sound of the wind was like the voice of some great loneliness that came up from the depths of the world.

She stood by the window, and she remembered the Sunday she had made her confirmation. How pretty she had been in her white dress! Yes, she had been a pretty girl. And how proud! How wonderful the world had been then! And now? No, the world was still wonderful. Lonely and poor as she was, she was here in this great and rich and free country, and she loved it. She would love it as much as she loved her own Poland.

And God loved her here as He had in Europe. God had looked after her on four continents. He was always there, there to watch over her. She was a child of God, and of Mary, and this would always sustain her wherever she was. She turned from the window to get ready for bed.

As Teresa began to undress, a sudden splitting headache made her wince. She wanted to cry out but she didn't. Her head throbbed. Her ears were stabbed with a sharp ache. Then the pains came in her legs.

She slowly undressed, went to the bathroom, brushed her teeth, washed her hands and face, and came out to go to bed. Her pretty face was contorted as she felt another stab of pain. She stood in the center of the room, fixed for a moment. She heard Julia's even breathing. Julia hadn't gotten these attacks, these pains in a German camp. A deep and fierce hatred of the Russians burned in her. As long as she lived, she would hate the Russians. Then she felt weak and impotent. Her pain continued.

Slowly she walked over to the couch, which served also as a bed, and knelt down to say her evening prayers.

Finishing her prayers, she rose, turned out the lights

and slipped into bed. She heard the wind against the windows. Her headache and earache began to ebb.

It had been, she decided, a good name-day, and there would be better name-days in the years to come here in America.

Teresa fell asleep.

Grammar School Love

Jack's fourteen-year-old brother Eddie stole some telephone slugs, and he and Jack got the idea that they would have some fun calling storekeepers and businessmen on the phone and giving out fake orders. They called a brewery and ordered a keg of beer for Mrs. Kew, who lived in the flat downstairs and who was supposed to be a Prohibitionist. Then they called up the Presbyterian minister and asked him to come right over to see Mrs. Kew because she was seriously ill and afraid that she might even die. They telephoned drugstores and ordered quarts of ice cream. They sent taxicabs on wild goose chases. Eddie spoke gruffly to an undertaker, saying he was Mr. Kennedy, the husband of the cranky old woman across the hall. He wanted him to come right over to get her body and have it prepared for burial. He talked as if he were going to spend a lot of money on the funeral. They had lots of fun doing all this. Both of them would have real funny stories to tell the kids they palled around with in school.

"Let's call up your girl Margie," Eddie suggested in a moment when they were wondering who else to phone.

Jack wanted to. It would be awful nice to hear her voice over the phone. But he knew Eddie. Eddie had teased him before, and in front of the whole family, too. Eddie always made a fool of him before everybody. Eddie would say something to Margie that might queer him with her forever. And he didn't stand in with her any too good as it was. He was afraid that Margie didn't like him much. He was always shy, not able to say anything in her presence, and most of the time when he passed her on the street, they didn't even say hello to each other. He told Eddie not to make the call. But Eddie was always picking on him anyway. Jack wished he was fourteen instead of twelve, so that he could clean the dickens out of his bullying brother. Eddie called up Margie. Jack protested, but what did Eddie care? Maybe, Jack thought and hoped, maybe Eddie wouldn't queer him this time. He asked Eddie, begging, not to say anything that would queer him.

"Hello, Margie? Margie, this is Eddie, Jack Malloy's brother. Yeh . . . he loves you, but he's afraid to say. so," Eddie said into the telephone.

Jack stood by, defeated and hurt. His face was a tragedy. Eddie was only telling her the truth. But what would she think? He had always wanted to say that to her, but he couldn't. His love for her was something he kept sacred inside of himself, something like an altar light always burning in church. It was part of himself that he kept secret and beautiful. And Eddie had spoiled it. He silently and bitterly cursed his older brother.

"No! No! . . . Cut it out, I tell you. . . . You're goin' too far. Cut it out. . . . Don't believe it, Margie. . . . Damn you, Eddie! I'll kill you," Jack shouted

"Do you hear him hollering, Margie?"

Jack hit Eddie in the ear with the heavy telephone directory. Then he flung a book, and it caught Eddie between the eyes. Eddie dropped the phone and rushed at Jack. They yelled at each other and cursed. Jack dodged as Eddie chased him around the circular table, but Eddie finally trapped him in a corner. Jack twisted away from his brother, sidestepped, and held out his foot. Eddie was spilled on his face.

Jack rushed up and grabbed the telephone.

"Hello . . . Hello . . . Listen . . . Margie, this is Jack . . . Don't believe my brother. . . . He's a damn liar."

He heard her laugh. And then, hearing the click of the receiver was something awful. But he didn't have time to think how really awful it was, because Eddie descended on him, punched him in the jaw and beat him up mercilessly.

On Sunday morning, Jack saw Margie. He was on his way home after having gone to nine o'clock mass, and she was on her way to ten o'clock mass. She wore a pink dress, and she was as prettily starched and all-around nice as a sweetheart in a story book. Seeing her made his nerves jumpy. He didn't know what he'd do or say. He was tongue-tied. He couldn't think of what he ought to do. He wondered—could she understand things? Could she? If only! If only she could see that he had feelings which were holy and he wanted to keep locked up inside himself like sacred things. He wondered if he ought to apologize for swearing, or what he ought to do or say. If only? Gee!

"Hello there, booby!"

He blushed. He grinned weakly, dispiritedly. He stood before her, abject. He felt awkward and out-of-place. She lifted her nose, and minced on past him.

She called back: "How's Mr. Pie-face this morning?"

He was afraid to turn and look at her. He walked on slowly, trying to act like he didn't care. When he did glance around, she was half a block away, walking as if she had never seen him. He seemed all shriveled up inside, like he was a dying flower lying on the ground where it was all cold and weedy. He didn't pay attention to where he was. It didn't matter. It would be just the same if a truck ran over him, or if it didn't.

Booby! Pie-face! She didn't care for him at *all*. He wished he were dead. But death was a terrible thing, icy and wormy, and not warm or soft at all. But it didn't matter. If he were dead, he wouldn't be any worse off. He would go on loving her like she was sacred while he lived . . . but she didn't care nothing at all for him. Death was terrible. . . . He walked along and he brooded.

Maybe it was his shyness. Maybe she thought his shyness was being afraid. Well, he was afraid of girls. He could lick any guy in his class, but she had him like a whipped puppy when she got scornful and looked at him mean. When he saw her he was a gawk, not saying a word, feeling worse than if he'd been out in the wet and was sopping, and all the while thinking of her niceness and his love for her. He loved her so much he could kneel down and pray to her.

And it was all Eddie's fault this time. There was a

name he wanted to call his brother, but he didn't dare to because it would be really an insult to his mother and not to Eddie. Well, he, Jack Malloy, would square things. His face became determined. He made his expression look hard and tough and rough. He was going to get even. He determined that someday, someday something would happen, and then all of them, even Margie, were going to feel bad for not understanding him.

He walked in Jackson Park. He had a lot of things to think about. The grass was all fresh like love. There were trees and birds and people everywhere. He listened to the birds sing and chirp, and he watched them play. The sparrows were noisy like some of the old ladies on his block. But the robins were nice, and the bluebirds were like Margie. He felt like he would like to have stolen the song of the birds and kept it, making it part of himself. He looked down at the lagoon. It was silver and gold and blue, and the sunlight on it was dancing. A lively collie was circling about near the bank, barking happily at his master. He watched the dog. He always felt that he wanted to talk with dogs because when they liked you, their faces had such a melting, understanding look. Maybe if dogs could talk they would know a lot of things.

He again determined that he would get even. You bet! He imagined that the happy dog was mad and that Margie was in its path. Then he would get even.

It would be a summer day, all gluey with heat. Margie would be walking down a lonely street. It would be like a terrible street in one of Sax Rohmer's stories. She wouldn't know that he was in back of her. Suddenly, a mad bulldog would come along, barking worse than if it was a crazy maniac talking. The dog's mouth would be foaming with white poison. Margie would be right in its path. She would see the dog and scream. The dog would go for her, and she would scream again; she would scream loud and terrible. She would be so afraid that she would stand like stone, not moving an inch. There she would be, and there would be the mad dog going for her. It would be a terrible thing, seeing that beautiful girl in a pink dress there, so frightened and helpless, and a mad dog, with a face worse than Battling Nelson's and foam coming out of its mouth, coming straight for her. And knowing that she couldn't do anything but get bitten, she would scream, and her scream for help would tear a person's heart right out. It would be awful, worse than a Chinaman murdering an American in one of Sax Rohmer's stories. The dog would come and leap . . . But just as the dog leaped, he would dive and make a flying tackle on the dog, hitting him harder than Shorty Des Jardin of the University of Chicago ever hit a fullback. He and the dog would roll over on the sidewalk, and there would be shouting and screaming and snarling and snapping, and the dog would be barking, making noises worse than the roar of a lion. He would sink his nails into the dog's throat, but would not get a good hold. The dog would squirm and twist free, and it would sink its poisonous fangs in his leg. He would not holler out, though it would hurt more than the time that lousy horse doctor on Sixty-third Street almost broke his jaw yanking a molar. He and the dog would roll over, and the dog would hang onto his thigh, and Margie, watching how brave he was in saving her, would be crying and frightened and praying for him and sorry because she had not understood him but had called him a boob and a pie-face. She would be so sad that no words would be able to describe how sorry she was. Finally, he would grab the dog's hind legs and, painfully getting to his feet, with his face a mask of pain and determination, he would twist the legs outward until the dog's teeth opened and loosed their death grip. Then, holding its legs, he would whirl and whirl, gathering speed and force, until he let the dog fly off on a tangent so that it would smash its head against a brick wall. Then he would look at Margie, proud and brave and silent. His expression would tell her all. It would tell her what kind of a boob he was. She would move toward him, but with a simple gesture of the left hand he'd stop her. He'd turn and walk away, his trouser leg ripped, sopped with his brave blood.

Once he'd heard from some grownup that if you were bitten by a mad dog, you went mad, you got hydrophobia, and you barked, snapped, foamed at the mouth, acted and tried to bite people like you were a mad dog yourself. When you got that way, there was no cure for you. They had to shoot you. Once he'd heard that there had been a boy on the West Side who'd been bitten by a mad dog, and the police had to kill him, so they tied a clothesline about his arms and legs and smothered him with a blanket.

Jack didn't want to die. But it would serve them all right because of the way he had been treated. Margie, everybody, would feel sorry. She would be sad and she would cry and cry and cry and cry. He saw how it would all be. Himself tied up with a clothesline, smothering between two thick blankets, writhing, barking, biting the blanket, choking for air, worse than if he had been caught in a burning building. Eddie, crying, hollering: "Gee, Jack, I'm sorry I ever picked on you, honest." Himself only barking and choking, suffocating, dying. Himself gaspy and almost smothered, ard Margie coming into the room, crying, her blue eyes sad and red with tears, her voice broken and she saying: Jack! . . . Jack! . . . Jack! . . . I'm sorry . . . I'm . . . I'm . . . I'm sorry . . . Oh! . . . Oh! . . . Please, Jack . . . don't die . . . I LOVE YOU!

And himself dying.

But dying was so terrible. Death was a bony old man seven feet tall with a face like the night when it is November and the wind is loud and there isn't any light in the sky. And his hands were icy, and his breath was like a blast from the North Pole. Death was terrible. But he didn't care. He would die and they'd be sorry. Himself dying like that, and Margie sobbing away. It would serve her right.

He walked on, and felt like a person who had suddenly wakened in a strange place. There were people and birds and dogs, and the sun was on the lagoon. He was always pretending to do things, pretending to get even, and nothing ever came out of his pretending. If he wasn't twelve years old and the toughest guy in his class, he would have cried.

I'm Dancing Frances

She was thin, almost slight, and had reddish-gold hair. She was also freckled. She was a pretty girl and her movements were lively. Sometimes she brought breakfast in to me, and every morning she cleaned my room and made the bed. She used to chat in a rich, full Irish brogue. She was very cheerful, smiled a lot and did her work well, except that she was slow because she spent so much time talking.

I'd be writing in my room when she came in, but I'd always stop and listen to her.

"And how are you this morning?" she'd always say. Then she would go to the bed and start making it. But she would stop, sometimes with a pillow in her hand, and she'd be off telling me something about the hotel or a guest.

"I don't like the South Africans," she said one morning. I turned around from the desk. She was holding a pillow in her hand. "They came in last night."

"Who did?"

"The South Africans. They're a dirty lot."

"Are they?"

"Are they! I wish they'd go to another hotel. The Americans aren't dirty like the South Africans. But we get all kinds of people here. They come from all over the world. And I say there's good and bad in all kinds. But I don't like the South Africans. They're a dirty lot. They're all sleepin' now." She smoothed the pillow and went on making the bed.

She would work and go on chatting away in her rich, soft brogue, and when she had finished arranging the room, she would stand in the center and talk, possibly as long as a half hour. She heard about almost everything that happened in the hotel, and she always had some bit of gossip or some reminiscences of a guest who had come and gone. She judged guests principally on whether or not they were clean and on their dispositions. She herself was very friendly, and she repeatedly said that she was a friendly person, and she liked the guests to be friendly. She didn't like the sour ones and would tell me, giving the number of the room occupied, about any guest who was sour.

"We're ordered to report if any guest has a lady with him all night," she told me, standing in the center of the room. "Every one of us is. They tell us to try and get in the rooms in the morning to see. If we don't report it, we might get sacked. They always are after us on that so as they can get their rates. Everyone working for the hotel watches. If a woman goes up in the elevator with a man at night, we hear about it, and we are ordered to find out if she spent the night in his room. They're fierce about that, not that they care what goes on, but they'll make the guest pay."

She told me more about this, describing in detail how the hotel employees watched. The hall porter, the elevator men and the maids were all required to report immediately in any case where a guest kept someone in his or her room for the night; and if this happened, the rate for the guest sleeping in the room for the night was put on the bill. The maids were ordered to look in all of the rooms every morning, and to nose around for any evidence that might indicate that there might have been an unpaying guest in one of the rooms. She told me about this with a sparkle of amusement in her blue eyes.

And she would talk about other things in the hotel. She lived here, and said that her quarters were bad but she preferred them to living at home. Her father was a workman, born in Ireland, and she had two younger sisters. They were all paying for a home and she contributed something out of the three pounds and nine shillings a week she earned toward making this payment.

"They all depend on Frances," she said. "If anything goes wrong or they are having any trouble, it's me they come to. It's always Frances. If my dad is sick, it's me he is wanting to see and take care of him."

"Do you like it here in England?"

"I like it. I love to dance. I'm Dancing Frances. That's me, Dancing Frances." She took several dance steps around the room and waved her arms. She seemed pathetic and sad to me as she danced.

Frances worked a split shift, in the morning and again in the evening, and she had already told me enough about her life for me to know that it was hard.

"Yes, I'm Dancing Frances," she said. Her eyes were brighter when she said this. She seemed very pretty. Her freckled face became more animated. And I wondered what dreams and wishes and fantasies were behind these words. "I love to dance," she told me as she stopped twisting about the center of the room.

"When do you dance?"

"Oh, in the afternoons when I'm off," she answered, but she didn't speak convincingly.

"Do you have a fellow?"

"No," she answered quickly. "I'm not hankering after getting married with the family needing me and depending on me. It's me they always come to." She stood in the center of the room for a moment with nothing more to say.

"I have to be getting on with me work, or they'll be raising the Ned with me."

She hurried out of the room.

The day before I left England on the trip when I'd met Frances, I took her to lunch. I met her in front of the hotel. She wore a gray suit of rough quality and of poor material. She looked shabby.

We had lunch in a tea-roomish place near Hyde Park. She spoke easily in a chatty sort of way, telling me more of her family. Her father was a good man. He didn't drink, but he was very bossy and always wanted his way. He hadn't liked it that she had left home and lived in the hotel, but she was working and bringing in money. Her quarters were small and, in fact, all she had was a little room like a cell. And the food she and the other maids ate was bad, too. She had to spend part of her weekly earning to supplement what she was fed by the hotel. What she was telling me at lunch, added to what she had already said at other times when she was cleaning and arranging my room, made it clear to me that hers was, materially, a bare and cheerless life. She worked fifty hours a week, and she gained very little from it for herself. Yet she was very cheerful and pleased that she could work.

And she spoke again of Ireland. "I'll never be wanting to go back there, except on a holiday if I have the money —sure, and there's nothing to do there. Sure, there's no excitement in Ireland."

"And is London exciting?"

Her eyes brightened. "That it is. Here I'm Dancing Frances," she said lightly, waving her arms at her side as she spoke. Then she spoke about her job. She liked it and she didn't like it. She would like to get a better situation. If she could, for instance, get a job as a maid or doing housework in a private home, that would please her very much.

After we ate, we took a walk in Hyde Park. A child had been born to Princess Elizabeth, and soldiers in the red uniforms of the Buckingham Guard were at the far end of the field. Cannons were to be shot heralding the birth of the royal child. We took chairs and sat watching the ceremonies. I asked her if she were cold, and she said that she wasn't. She seemed chilled. She wanted to stay and watch the ceremonial parade of the Horse Guard and to hear the cannon shots go off.

People passed and we looked at them idly.

I casually reflected on the accident of circumstances. My own grandmother had been Irish-born and she might have been an Irish girl like this one sitting beside me in Hyde Park. My grandmother had gone to America and had worked as a domestic. Domestic service in a London home would delight this Irish girl. If her parents or grandparents had gone to America, her life should have been different, and she shouldn't be wearing this cheap, shabby suit and thinking that the long hours she would work in some rich home would be such an improvement for her over the long hours she now worked in a big London hotel.

"Sure, the English are a strange people, aren't they?"

"Why?"

"All this fuss over a baby born."

I smiled.

Far down on the green, we could see the cannon and the red uniforms of the Buckingham Guard. People were lining up along the edges of the long and wide rectangular stretch of green and waiting patiently.

"It doesn't mean anything to you?" I asked her.

"Sure, and what doesn't?"

"The ceremony and the birth of a royal prince—or is it a princess?"

"I wouldn't be knowin' if the baby's a boy or a girl."

It began to drizzle again. The dark sky and the vague mist in the air brought out the Irish green colors of the park. It was August, but the smell and chill of autumn were in the air.

Soon the Horse Guards paraded, and we joined the line of people watching. They wore their large dark beaver hats and red coats, and their swords clanked as they drew up in the center of the field. The cannon went off. Thirty shots were fired, slowly, and puffs of smoke drifted into the dark sky, far down the park. Around us were interested, even solemn faces. And, also, I noticed that, by American standards, many of those about were poorly dressed.

The ceremony ended. The soldiers left. The crowd moved away. It was still drizzling. I walked out of the park with Frances and said good-by to her in front of the hotel.

Instead of giving her a tip, I promised to send her nylon stockings from America. I sent them but never learned whether or not she received them. I tried through an American friend to get her a domestic job in an American home in London. I was unsuccessful. The next time I was in London, she was no longer working at the hotel. I wonder what has happened to her.

Memento Mori

Milt Coggswell never really enjoyed himself. When he was a skinny young man, he got a job driving an express wagon. He worked on wagons for years before he was promoted to the supervision. Then as a route inspector, he worked hard, although not so hard as he did on the wagons.

Milt came from the southwest side of Chicago. His father, a carpenter, had been a heavy drinker and died penniless. As a boy and a young man, Milt had been quiet. He had seemed to be very self-contained. He rarely got into trouble or into fights with the other boys. They didn't pick on him much. They didn't think of him very much. If he was around, he was included in their games and pranks. If he was absent, no one noticed the fact. He was neither well liked nor disliked. He was accepted as someone who is vaguely there.

Milt didn't seem to be too troubled when his father came home drunk. He said little about it and gave little evidence that it affected him. His father, even in fits of drunkenness, rarely menaced him. The old man usually became sentimental when he was in his cups, and many of his drunks turned into crying jags. This was distasteful to young Milt, but it didn't evoke any unusual feeling. He wished his father weren't such a man. He had two brothers and two sisters, and he got on well with them. But he exchanged no confidences with any of them. He held his own against them if they tried to impose on him, as he held his own if his father happened to act unpleasantly. Once when the old man was about to rush on him, Milt, then a boy of thirteen, quietly told his father not to hit him. His father didn't.

After graduating from grammar school, it was ex-

pected that he would go to work. His first job was that of
an errand boy. Then he got a job as an office boy for a
wholesale hardware company. After losing that during
a lay-off at a time when business was bad, he looked day
after day for work, and finally got his job on a wagon.

He went about his business as a young expressman. He
talked to the people with whom he came in contact. They
talked to him. He did his work conscientiously, but he
was never criticized by his fellow workers as one who
spoiled the job for others. He was all right with them. He
would, now and then, stop in a saloon on the way home
from work and have a few beers. Beer didn't seem to
have much effect on him. He never drank enough to become drunk. He drank several glasses of beer as though
he were drinking water. He would, in the saloon, smile at
jokes, listen to dirty stories and even, to some extent,
participate in the railery. But he didn't seem to enjoy this
either. He never would let go in belly laughs. He never
would get truly angry. Even when he went to brothels he
didn't seem to become excited. He didn't talk of the
pleasures and thrills he expected, as some of the other
men would, and after he came from the brothel, he didn't
talk of the girl, the excitement, the joys he had, as-
sumedly, experienced. He listened to others talk of the
girls, and would sometimes say that his had been good.
But there was no enthusiasm in what he said.

He began courting a plain-looking girl named Evelyn
when he was twenty-three. But even courtship didn't
seem to rouse him to any pitch of emotion. He liked the
girl and kept seeing her and taking her out. He sent her
a card on St. Valentine's Day. He gave her Christmas
presents and a present on her birthday. He took her out
steadily, three nights a week. He talked to her about
himself, his work, his family, the weather, shows they
saw together, picnics they attended, parties and dances
and songs, but always in the same unenthusiastic way.
Everything seemed equal in meaning. He talked of love
pretty much as he did of the weather. He kissed and
hugged this girl, but then he would seem slightly stiff and
proper, unmoved. He proposed to her in a calm voice.
He seemed to take her acceptance as a matter of course.

Then he planned the future with his fiancée. They discussed the home they would have, the furniture they would buy, the things they would do. He was sensible and clear-headed. When he and his fiancée went to look at furniture, he revealed a sound sense of money value. But he didn't really enjoy what he was doing.

Milt, himself, didn't seem aware of the fact that he never enjoyed life. He imagined that he did. He imagined that people were all pretty much the same as he was. When he saw anyone get angry or heard someone talking with verve and spirit, he didn't compare such conduct with his own. He sometimes got a little sore, and he imagined that it was the same with others. He was unaware of any such thing as excessive emotion, passion, intensity. Life was just a matter of routines and habits to him. It had always seemed to be that way. He had never known a time when it wasn't. Even as a child, he had been good and had not given his mother much trouble. That was the way he had always been.

It was no different with his religion. Milt was a Catholic. He believed—or rather, he didn't disbelieve. He didn't think about his religion. He was a passingly good Catholic. He attended Mass regularly, and two or three times a year he received Holy Communion. He was always on time at Mass, and while it was being celebrated he would pray silently at a kind of slow tempo. He said prayers by rote, and as he did, he would think of the literal meanings of the words of the "Hail Mary" and of the "Our Father." He thought, in a very simple way, of the appearance of Heaven, God, and Mary. He imagined that Mary looked exactly like the plaster statue of the Blessed Virgin in his parish church.

Milt was fond of saying that he took life as it came, and this epitomized the full meaning of life for him. He didn't get excited and he didn't worry. He ate, but not too much. One food was much the same to him as another. One type of enjoyment was much the same as another. One friend would do just as well as any other friend. One day was like another day. Everything was like everything else to him, and pleasures and people were as though interchangeable. He didn't think much of the past, and he didn't think much of the future. He did save money every week, but he didn't do it with any great fear of the future. He just saved and would say that, after all, a man ought to save a little for a rainy day because when it rained, you needed an umbrella. His savings account was like an umbrella. He had a savings account just as he owned a pair of rubbers which he wore if it was wet outside.

He wasn't unduly excited at his own marriage. Others had gotten married before him. Others would get married after him. You got married just as you got up in the morning, had breakfast, and went to work. It was part of life. He was glad to be getting married. It would be comfortable. His wife would take care of him, and it was a good idea to have a woman sc that when you wanted her, you had her. That was what a woman was for. She was part of the scenery of a man's life. She was to be had. You married her to have her.

Milt seemed like a happily married man, and he would have been one if he had been a happy man. But life didn't mean enough to him for him to enjoy it. Neither did it mean enough to him for him to be miserable. He took life for granted. He took himself for granted. He took his wife for granted. He never speculated about life and death. He never wondered what his wife was like. She was like what she was. She enjoyed seeing moving pictures, and he went to moving pictures with her. She preferred ten o'clock Mass on Sundays and so, when he was not working on a Sunday, they went to ten o'clock Mass. She liked to cook certain kinds of food, and so he ate what she cooked for him. She was available to him, and when he wanted her, they didn't talk about it. He just took her to bed. Or if she felt that way, she would come up to him and kiss him and he would know, and without a word he would take her into the bedroom. Then he forgot it, just as he forgot her the moment he left home on his way to work, and just as he forgot work the moment he was finished for the day and went back home for his supper. And Evelyn seemed to be very much like him. She, too, thought that she was happy and that she was having a good life. She had a man who provided for her, left her alone about the management of her home, never questioned what she did, gave her what she needed for groceries and other household items, and they rarely quarreled.

They talked quite a bit. He always spoke of the weather. He told her how he felt and would speak of the day at work, and she would tell him what she did, how much she had paid for groceries, whom she had seen shopping, and about the weather. They both had a capacity for talking about such matters at length, and when they did, almost nightly, they spoke with no emphasis in what they said, no use of words which would suggest anything singular and peculiar to themselves. They might have been two other people talking about the weather and about various commonplace details of ordinary life. Frequently they would talk about what they read in the newspapers, the misfortunes, the crimes, the tragedies which were printed daily, discussing them in much the same way as they commented on the weather.

Thus had life gone on for Milt Coggswell.

When Evelyn became pregnant, no changes came in the tone of their relationship. He came home from work one day and she told him the news, and he said that he was glad of it and hoped that their child would be a son. But he said this in much the same way as he said, immediately afterward, that it had been a nice warm day. Evelyn quickly began to prepare for the coming event. Before she was three months' pregnant, she had already done a great deal of knitting for the baby. Her pregnancy was, on the whole, an easy one. Milt came home every night and asked her how she felt, very much in the same way he asked her whether she thought it had been a good day. She would answer him, but she might just as well have answered him by saying that the sun had or had not been shining.

The child was a boy. Milt liked this, but he wasn't excited. He passed out cigars at work, and wheeled the baby carriage on Sunday, and now and then played with the infant. But again, he didn't do this with any depth of interest. For he was incapable of possessing any depth of interest about anything in this world. The child was well-cared for, and two others, a boy and a girl, also arrived in due time. And the life of this family went on in an uneventful way. There were few quarrels. The children were raised as other children were. The administrations of punishment were left to the father. Milt would spank when Evelyn thought it was necessary, but he might just as well have been shaving himself or sweeping off the front porch. He spanked methodically and didn't hit too hard, and yet he hit with sufficient force to sting the children and evoke tears.

They began to look for a house to buy, saved their money, and eventually found a house out near Madison and past Western. It was a two-story brick house about ten years old, and it was clean and comfortable, and they kept it that way. They rented the second floor to a chief clerk in a drug company, and had no difficulties with their tenants. Now and then the two families talked together. The children played together, and the wives watched the children for one another when it was necessary. Life went on thus, and time passed.

In good weather and when there was nothing else to do, Milt would, after dinner, sit on the back porch and look off at the sky, saying little, just gazing. He would sometimes sit this way for half an hour or more. His wife often sat with him. When she did, they would exchange an occasional word, and they would both sit, looking around, gazing at the grass, the rear of other buildings and at the sky. Sometimes Milt would play a few games of solitaire and whenever he won, he told his wife. She would congratulate him. They would go to bed early.

But when Milt was approaching forty, he began to have stomach aches. At first he paid no attention to them, thinking that any man can now and then get a stomach ache. But the aches and pains continued. He would have pains fairly often before his meals, and he would fill with gas, have heartburn, and get a nauseous taste in his mouth. At first he didn't go to a doctor, but went to the druggist instead and got various medicines that the druggist recommended. These did no good. Still he didn't go to a doctor. He didn't believe that anything was wrong with him.

But as time went on and the pains persisted, Milt began to worry. In fact, he began to worry seriously for the first time in his life. He would wake up in the morning, worried and a little frightened, waiting in suspense to learn whether he would have any pain or stomach discomfort. He would interrupt his reading of the morning newspaper on the streetcar, look up blankly at the ceiling and wonder frettingly if he were ill, if he were in any danger. At work he began to talk more about food, and would ask questions of the other men, questions about what they ate, their digestion, their bowel habits and the like. He watched others eat, noted what they ordered, looked at food on the plates of strangers. He was becoming fearful about food.

At first he had said nothing to Evelyn. But as his condition recurred again and again, he told her. She put him on various diets. First she fed him more fresh vegetables. Then she gave him no vegetables. She also gave him mild cathartics and prunes. She asked him, each morning and night, how his stomach was and he always reported its condition to her. But since his trouble was periodic, he still didn't see a doctor and imagined that it would go away of its own accord.

Finally he passed a sleepless night, gripped by intense pains, at times doubled up. He had to exert all his will power in order not to moan. In the morning he was very weary, but he had no pains. So he spent a fatigued day at work, came home in more pain and distress, and that night went to a doctor who had an office over a drugstore two blocks from his home. The doctor examined him carefully and found nothing specific to diagnose. He told Milt not to worry. The doctor gave him a prescription for pills, a sedative which he was to take before every meal. He was also instructed to rest a half hour before each meal, but Milt told him that he couldn't do this except at dinnertime and on Sundays. So the doctor told him to do this when he could. The doctor also told him that if he took it easy, rested, didn't worry, he wouldn't have to be concerned and his condition would undoubtedly clear up.

As Milt left the doctor's office, he had a strange

thought. He wondered if there were something seriously the matter with him. But this thought dropped out of his mind. He went on home, and dully told Evelyn what the doctor had said. Evelyn said that she would see to it that he rested and that she would plan to have their suppers a half hour later so that he could take a nap when he came home from work. She didn't seem to be overly concerned about his condition, and accepted what the doctor said as gospel truth. He went on in his usual way, following the doctor's instructions as closely as the circumstances of his life permitted. When he had lunch with route inspectors and wagon dispatchers from the express company and took his sedative before lunch, they would rag him about it. They would say that the company was getting him, and that that was what happened when you worried. One said that that was what happened when a route inspector tried to sit on the lap of Joe Leonard, the assistant superintendent, who was Milt's immediate boss. Another told him that he was too old to be going off half cocked over some young jane, and still another said that all that Milt was capable of was to go off half cocked over a jane. Milt took this raillery and replied, but his own sallies were pretty commonplace. He told them that the pills restored him, and someone said that then the doc must have given Milt monkey-gland pills.

Now and then, as more time passed, that same thought recurred in Milt's mind. Was there really something wrong with him? He was well past forty now. He showed signs of age. His hair was getting gray, and his face had grown thinner. His face was becoming lined. He felt that perhaps there was really something wrong with him. He had no appetite any more, and his stomach condition kept recurring. But the doctor kept assuring him that it was only nerves. Milt's stomach became a standing joke among the expressmen.

He was closest to Bohunk August, who was short and fat and had an outgoing personality. August and he often ate together, and since they had adjoining routes on the West Side, they would ride out to their routes together in the afternoon after lunch. Milt finally talked to August about his stomach, his pains and aches, his pills, his gas, and his constipation. August always listened sympathetically and privately guessed that there must be something wrong at home between Milt and his wife, but he never said this to Milt. August was notorious among the expressmen for bumming and cadging cigarettes instead of smoking his own, but Milt always willingly extended his pack to him. He considered August his best friend, but there was no real closeness between them. Never in his life had Milt been close to any other human being.

Now, as he approached fifty, he was too concerned with his own stomach and the question as to whether or not there was anything really wrong for him to be able to feel any closeness. He had no other problems but his stomach. His children had grown up. The boys were working, and his daughter was married to a steady, hardworking mechanic. His wife seemed contented. She was a bit stout, but her health was good. She and Milt still talked as they always had, but they also talked about food and his stomach. He was satisfied with his job, and he expected to be working at it until he retired. They had saved money, and their house was almost paid for. He had no unfulfilled ambitions. He liked to hear the radio and spent long periods at night listening; this passed the time for him. He was getting along. There was food on the table. He did have pains and gas and constipation from time to time, but he never lost much time from work, and now and then, when he did have to lay off or when he was in bed with a cold, he got paid. Considering his ambition, his character, his education, Milt was in good circumstances. But he still wondered if there was something wrong with him.

And he had aged noticeably. He looked about ten years older than his actual years. He was quite thin, and he was gray. His face was wrinkled and pinched. There were blotches of red on it, and sometimes strangers or acquaintances thought he was a dissipated old boozer. He looked like a man who had never gotten one moment of joy out of his entire life.

The men who were growing old with him at the express company, who were starting to get bald, to get fat, to feel the beginning of a loss of their grip on life, and whose hair was turning gray—they all noticed how Milt had changed in appearance. However, they rarely said anything to him of it except in their kidding remarks, and many of these related to women. Yet they noticed. They all thought they would outlive him.

Thus had been Milt's life. Then on Christmas Day in 1931, Milt was scheduled to work down in the Wagon Department. He and his wife got up very early. There was a blizzard. Looking out of the window, Milt remarked that it was real Christmas weather, a white Christmas. His wife said that it was too bad that he had to work, but that since he was working, they would have their turkey dinner at about seven-thirty and that she did hope that his stomach would be all right so that he could eat his fill. They dressed to go to Mass together. They had gone to Mass together for years now; the idea of not going never occurred to them. Even though there was a blizzard, it did not occur to Evelyn that she need not go to such an early Mass with him. So they dressed warmly. Milt put on rubbers, a warm muffler and ear laps. They left the house and plodded through the snow, not complaining, taking the snow and the blizzard and even their discomfort as much for granted as they had taken nearly everything in their lives. As they crossed a street, unable to see in the blinding and whirling snow, they were both knocked down by an automobile. Evelyn died on the way to the hospital. Milt passed away a few hours later.

The day after the funeral, McGinty, working at his Tractor Board of the Wagon Department, suddenly turned around to look at the others in the office and said dolefully: "Jesus, that was certainly tough on Milt Coggswell."

"Well, death sure is a funny thing, and none of us know how we're going to get it," said Les Crady, one of the clerks.

"You know, now that is certainly a surprise. Here Milt and his wife go out to early Mass on Christmas mornin' and they're crossing the street when along comes an automobile and keels the two of them right over," said McGinty.

"Anyway they had the priest. They died right," said Les.

"Yeah, that was good," said McGinty, shaking his head sadly.

"You know, I sometimes wonder about life. It's a funny thing, the way life goes on. It's damn funny. You know, Casey, it's damn funny," another clerk said.

"As a fellow lives, many strange things happen—like Milt getting knocked down by an automobile on Christmas morning and dying. You know, that could happen to any one of us. It could happen to me or you. Did you ever think of that?" said Coco, a new clerk.

"Yeah," said Les.

"Milt was a good expressman," McGinty said.

Then the route inspectors started coming into the Department from eleven o'clock on, and they all talked about Milt.

Bohunk August got their attention and said: "Jesus, you know, when I left the office with Milt the day before Christmas. I never thought it would be the last time I would see him. I was telling him that when you had stomach troubles, the important thing to watch was getting out the stuff that you put in. And he was telling me what he was giving his grandchild for Christmas, and how he planned to have a nice Christmas dinner. He was telling me how he had to work the Christmas before. Now, I'd never have thought that it would be the last time that I was gonna see Milt. Poor Milt! . . . Say, Mac, got a cigarette? I forgot to buy a pack."

McGinty sneered at August and said: "I can see why you're sorry Milt got killed. You won't get any more free cigarettes."

Then they started kidding August because he cadged cigarettes, and they forgot about Milt Coggswell.

Senior Prom

When ten different girls had turned him down for a date for the Alumni Dance in April, Danny was hurt and deeply embarrassed. He couldn't understand why girls wouldn't date him and wondered what was wrong with him. One of these girls had been Gertrude O'Sullivan, and three days after she had sweetly and politely refused Danny, she'd given a date to Ike Dugan. Danny and Mush were fraternity brothers, and Danny was sure that Gertrude would tell Mush of his phone call. He had had the same difficulty in getting dates before, and he had become convinced that many girls talked about him and laughed at him behind his back.

Marty Mulligan, Ike Dugan and his other fraternity brothers had talked a lot about their dates and the plans they had for the Alumni Dance, and this had only impressed on Danny a renewed sense of his own failure and his loneliness. He nursed a secret wound, which, in addition to the other shames he carried, distressed him. His father was poor, paralyzed, and dying. His Uncle Al was not doing too well and was unable to pay for his final year's tuition at St. Stanislaus. He wouldn't be able to go to college as would some of his classmates. Recognized as one of the star athletes of the school, he was beginning to look on this reputation with very critical eyes. An all-around sense of failure was gnawing within him. His inability to date girls and to win the affection of one who would love him and be his steady date was eating away his confidence.

He hadn't wanted to go to the Alumni Dance without a date, but he had gone out of sheer determination. It was held at the Warwick Hotel on Fifty-third Street. He'd gone there to his first dance a few months earlier, taking a dark-haired girl named Sheila Cullen, but she had refused to give him a second date. At the Alumni Dance, Danny had hung around with other stags, pretending to be casual and nonchalant and trying to act as though being a stag was what he had wanted. Marty Mulligan had given him a dance with his girl, Mary Boylan, and he'd been given two other dances by other fraternity brothers.

After the dance he had tagged along with the crowd going to the Bamboo Inn on Sixty-third Street, but feeling out-of-place. He'd danced once again with Mary Boylan. While the others were dancing, he'd stared out at the floor, moody and meditative. The music had roused desires for love in him. Trying to look philosophical and observant, he had been raw with a loneliness. He'd wished that he were blind drunk and able to show them all that he was somebody and that he didn't give two hoots in hell for anyone or anything. But that had not represented his real feeling. He wanted a girl and he wanted to be in love. And the orchestra played "My Wonderful One," and he had watched the dancers and had dreamed.

One day during the week after the dance, Emil Heiden came up alongside of Danny in the school yard at lunch hour and said: "Say, Goof, you're learning to dance like the cat's meow, but you couldn't date a broad that rates if you tried."

Even though Heiden was bigger than he was, Danny felt like swinging on him. But if he had, he'd only have made himself appear to be funnier. It would have been a dead giveaway of his feelings, and he'd have looked ridiculous before the entire student body. He didn't answer Heiden but determined that he would get a beautiful girl to take to the Senior Prom at the end of May. Since he was a senior, it would be his farewell. He made a pledge to himself, but not with any genuine confidence, that he would be successful. Still, this resolution soothed his hurt feelings. He dreaded the thought of being in the stag line again, smiling merely to conceal his humiliation. He told himself that he would show Big Heiden and everyone else in his class. He'd bow out at S.S. with a girl who would be considered the keenest girl at the Senior Prom. He wouldn't fail this time. He couldn't allow himself to.

One day he met Marion Shires on Fifty-eighth Street. He remembered her as Helen Shires's kid sister—a skinny little girl on Indiana Avenue—but now she had blossomed into a slender, sylphlike, beautiful, blond-haired girl. He wanted to be in love, and any beautiful girl would fulfill this need. It could be Marion, he thought. And if he took her to the Senior Prom, the boys would open their eyes and take notice. Gliding about the floor of the Warwick Hotel's Ball Room with her, he would cut a figure. She smiled at him on Fifty-eighth Street, said hello and asked how he was; he talked to her for a minute or two. He glanced after her and decided that he'd telephone Marion to invite her to go to the dance with him. He immediately imagined her accepting; then he thought of himself kissing her in a taxi on the way home. But strolling on toward South Park Avenue with a far-off look in his bespectacled eyes, his confidence flattened out; he feared the humiliation he would feel if she refused him.

For several days he thought and daydreamed of Marion, but hesitated telephoning her. Then, impulsively and with sudden resolution, he rushed into one of the telephone booths of the Walgreen Drug Store at Fifty-eighth Street and Prairie Avenue and gave the operator Marion's number. He had memorized it the day after he'd run into her.

He was tense when he heard her voice at the other end of the wire. It sounded cold and snooty.

"This is Danny O'Neill," he said in a quick, unsure gush.

"Oh!" she exclaimed, her voice suggesting disappointment.

For a moment, he didn't know what to say. There was despair inside him. He held the receiver to his ear. He couldn't talk of dates, dances, orchestras or jazz the way the other fellows did with girls. He had no line. He forced out a cough.

"What do you want?" she asked indifferently.

In a near panic, Danny knew he'd lost again.

"Well," he said dispiritedly, "our . . . my . . . class is

having a Senior Prom next month, and I just buzzed to ask if you'd care to go with me."

"When is it?"

"The last Friday in May," he answered with fresh hope.

"No, I have a date that night."

"Oh," he said in a sinking mood. He was speechless again and he didn't want to hang up. Even in the telephone booth he blushed. He had in this last year been turned down by girl after girl after girl.

"Perhaps some other time," Marion said, her voice less indifferent. "I'm very sorry, but thank you."

"I'm sorry, too, because it's going to be a pretty hot jig," Danny said, trying to sound nonchalant: he was imitating the way his fraternity brother, Wils Gillen, talked.

"What orchestra will you have?"

"Bensen's," he said, speaking like one who was in the know.

"It's good."

"Yeah—it's good." A little self-consciously he added, "Keen. They play some pretty hot tunes." Perhaps he was finding his tongue and making a good impression. She might break her other date and agree to go with him.

"Bensen's played at the Phi Psi formal at the Opera Club last week."

"I heard about it," he said with an air of importance. But then, there was an awkward pause. "Can't you break your date and come? It's going to be a nice hop that you oughtn't to miss, Marion."

"Oh, I couldn't do that."

"That's too bad," he said, trying again to seem casual and to mask his disappointment.

"I'm very sorry—but thanks awfully for calling."

He was speechless.

"Perhaps some other time," she said.

"Yes, maybe another time."

"Good-by."

He heard the receiver click. He walked out of the telephone booth feeling insignificant. All over again he believed that there must really be something wrong with him.

He walked dejectedly along Fifty-eighth Street toward South Park Avenue.

With the dance still almost four weeks off, Danny was worried. Marty Mulligan, Ike Dugan and his other fraternity brothers had already gotten dates. So had most of his classmates; even Shanley, who was the smartest fellow in class, had a date. Shanley wasn't fast with girls the way Danny pretended to be. Now and then, whenever there was any talk of the Senior Prom, Danny became defensively silent. He was haunted by the fear that he wouldn't get a date. His career at St. Stanislaus was just about finished, and what had he to look forward to? Despair was creeping through him. He believed that almost no one in his class seemed to have poorer prospects in life than he. He couldn't go to college and he had lost interest in study. He'd go into the Continental Express Company and follow in the footsteps of his sick father and his older brother. To show up without a date at the Senior Prom would be like placing the brand of failure upon himself. But it seemed that girls just didn't want to go with him. He imagined that they ticketed him as a dope and a bore. He believed that the fellows in his frat knew this and talked about it when he was not around. It was like carrying a scar that marked him off and set him apart from others.

As a grammar school kid he'd been called "Four Eyes" because of his glasses, and at times this had wounded him. He began to get troubled and self-conscious about his glasses. He passed along from one listless day to the next. A date with a pretty girl would seem like a redemption. He wanted to be seen at the dance with the most beautiful girl present. And he wanted this girl to fall in love with him. He wanted to love and to be loved, and his desire filled him with a desperation that kept sapping his already weakened confidence.

He resolved again and again to find a beautiful girl. But the list of possible girls whom he might call seemed to have been exhausted. He couldn't phone girls like Natalie O'Reedy or Gertrude O'Sullivan who had already turned him down two, three, and four times. And if he

asked one St. Paul girl and failed, then she might tell all
the other possible girls in the school, and he'd be cooked
with all of them. He thought that perhaps he might just
not go to the dance. He could tell the fellows that he had
a date, invent some name and then, on the night of the
prom, he could feign illness. He knew, however, that he
wouldn't do this. He had to go, and he had to find a girl.

Danny was ready to give up one night as he sat at the
dinner table with his Aunt Margaret, his Uncle Ned, and
his grandmother. He ate rapidly, almost wolfing down his
food. He was silent and moody. The name of Sis Hansen
came to his mind unexpectedly.

She was a freshman at Park High and only sixteen. He
was nineteen now. But she was fully developed, and fellows around the neighborhood always spoke extrava-
gantly about her beauty. Wils Gillen said that she was
like a beautiful doll. Milt Rosenplatz said that she was
like a Greek statue in the Art Institute and had the brains
of one. Danny didn't care about her brains. She was the
prettiest girl he could think of, the prettiest girl he knew.
But he hardly knew her. Still, that was all to the good.
She wouldn't know of his reputation, of his failures with
so many other girls. She wasn't Catholic and didn't know
the St. Paul girls or others who went with the fellows in
his bunch. He'd telephone her.

But he put off making the phone call for several days.
He sat in class daydreaming of Sis and trying to think
up a line that might impress her. He held imaginary conversations with her, and in his own eyes he seemed to be
very clever. But then he felt foolish and confused.

One evening about eight o'clock he went out because
he didn't want his folks to hear him calling a girl and
asking for a date. In the drugstore at Fifty-eighth Street
and Calumet Avenue he looked up her number and
telephoned. Hearing her voice, he didn't know what to
say nor how to lead up to asking her. He blurted out his
request and she said yes immediately.

Danny walked out of the booth grinning and full of
hope and confidence. He'd done it. And Sis Hansen
would be one of the prettiest, if not *the* prettiest girl at
the Senior Prom.

Danny immediately believed that he was in love with Sis Hansen. Over and over again he told himself that she was beautiful.

The next morning he felt like a different person as he went to school. He was young and healthy, and he believed that he shouldn't be so glum about himself and the future. And maybe Sis Hansen would love him, and they'd go out on steady dates, and he would work and develop great ambition and rise in the world, all for Sis's sake. He was probably the best all-around athlete in his class, and he had made his mark at school. He was somebody at S.S. now at the closing of his high school career. He walked into the brick schoolyard beaming with smiles, feeling like an important person.

"Hello, Dope," Marty Mulligan said, coming up to him.

"Hi!"

"Sell anyone tickets for the hop?"

"One—but say, I've got an idea."

"You better do something about it quick, O'Neill, before it dies of lonesomeness."

His idea was to sell tickets to two young baseball players on the Chicago Cubs who came from Massachusetts and were friends of Joe McBride, their football coach. These players had both been out to football and baseball practice of St. Stanislaus teams in Jackson Park. Marty told Danny that it would be a good idea if it worked.

Emil Heiden drifted up to join them and sarcastically asked Danny: "Got a date yet?"

"Yes," Danny answered very casually as he privately enjoyed a moment of great triumph.

"She can't be much if she goes to a dance with you," Heiden said.

"Wait and see," Danny said, still very casually.

"Who is she?" asked Marty.

"Her name's Sis Hansen. She lives in my neighborhood."

"I don't know her, but the name sounds familiar. I must have heard it somewhere," Marty remarked.

"She goes to Park High, and she's in the Sig chapter there," Danny said, still quite matter-of-fact.

"Sig?" Marty scratched his head. "Sig girls rate."

"If she rated, why would she be going out with him?" asked Emil Heiden.

"Listen, you lummox," Marty said, "you don't know this guy O'Neill. He dates a different girl for every one of our frat parties or dances, and he always comes up with a keen number."

Danny felt triumphant. Marty's defense of him would impress and put Heiden in his place. And now it wouldn't be a succession of keen girls, but only Sis. She would love and understand him, and that's what he wanted and needed. He'd found his girl. Danny grinned confidently.

Ralph Borax, who lived in the Fifty-eighth Street neighborhood, joined them.

"Got a date for the Prom?" Danny asked.

"Yeah—I'm taking Fritzie Lonigan."

"She's a swell girl," Danny said.

"Who are you taking, Dan?" Ralph asked.

"Sis Hansen."

"Do you know her, Borax? Is she hatchet-faced?" Marty asked.

"She's the most beautiful girl around Fifty-eighth Street," Ralph said enthusiastically. He shot his hand out at Danny. "Congratulations," he said as they shook.

"See, Heiden? What did I tell you about O'Neill?" Marty asked.

"She may be what Borax said, but I'm from Missouri, and even if Borax is right, then she's got holes in her head."

Father Michael rang the cowbell. Moving over to line up with the seniors, Marty said: "We won't be doing this much longer."

Sis Hansen was vivid and lovely in Danny's mind.

The coming dance and his date with Sis filled Danny's last days at St. Stanislaus with soft dreams. He counted the days until that of the Prom, and he lived for the moment when he would ring the doorbell in the apartment building at Fifty-ninth Street and South Park Avenue and then march up the stairs to her home. He thought of what he would first say to her. And this scene recurred again and

again in his daydreams. And he would take her to the
dance in a cab.

But he had another problem. He was poor. He'd need
from eight to ten dollars for the dance. There was two
dollars for the ticket, cab fares to the hotel, from the
hotel to the Bamboo Inn or some other place where the
bunch would go, and then a third cab in which to take
her home. And there would be the cost of ginger ale and
perhaps a chicken sandwich or something else to eat at
the Bamboo Inn. Some of the boys would chip in and
try to buy a bottle, but he'd stay out of that. He'd stay
completely sober for Sis. Here was his fate. How would
he ever find a girl more beautiful than Sis?

But he would need money. He got fifty cents a day for
lunch and he would have to save from that. Things were
going badly with his uncles. And there was his father at
home, paralyzed and, he feared, dying. He was often
ashamed that his family was poor and that he couldn't
keep up with the fellows in his frat. They all had more
spending money than he, and they were better dressed.
He couldn't let them know this or he'd be deeply hu-
miliated. And he couldn't seem cheap or poor when he
took Sis to the dance. If she knew that he was poor, she
might drop him. Even though he now had a date with
Sis, he was hurt. He was hurt because of his poor parents and because of the sinking fortunes of his uncles. He
was hurt with many little shames.

He didn't belong with Marty, Mush, Hugh McNeill.
They lived in happier and better and richer homes. Sometimes he felt like an imposter when he was with them.
And one night at a meeting, his frat brothers had lit into
him about his conduct with girls, about insulting them,
and the wisecracks he sometimes made when he'd been
turned down on dates. He'd done that because he was
hurt. And he did and said many things for the same
reason. But if a girl loved him—only him—and saw him
for what he was inside, he wouldn't feel so hurt. It would
be a compensation and a reward. And if that reward were
given him, the real Danny would come to the surface
and she, the girl who loved him, would know this real

Danny. He would love her, and there would be no end to what he would try to do for her.

And now that girl was going to be Sis Hansen. He hoped this. After the dance, in the cab and then in her hallway, he would kiss her, and the lips of Sis Hansen would awaken in him the real Danny O'Neill.

He saved from his lunch money. He went hungry. He continued to count the days until the night of the Senior Prom. All of his life centered on and pointed to that night. But never, he thought, had the days been so long.

And over and over in his mind the words of popular songs flowed as he waited in daydreams. Often he sang to himself:

"My wonderful one, whenever I'm dreaming love's delight,
  I'm dreaming of you.
  'Tis you I adore; 'tis you I implore."

Sis Hansen was "the wonderful one."

He had eight dollars. The ticket cost two and that left him six. This would be plenty for the night. He wore new shoes and a new suit he'd gotten for his graduation, two weeks off. His hair was slicked down with vaseline; he was shaved. And now his long wait was almost over. In an hour he'd ring Sis's doorbell, promptly at nine o'clock. And she'd look swell. He imagined the two of them entering the Warwick Hotel and crossing the lobby, and then he imagined her in his arms on the dance floor.

Beaming, he walked about to pass the time. He stopped in at the pool room near Fifty-eighth Street and the elevated station, and he saw Milt Rosenplatz. He told Milt that he was taking Sis to the dance. Milt grew enthusiastic about her beauty. This was like savoring his triumph in advance.

Then he left the pool room and walked about some more, wanting this last hour to pass. He grew nervous and excited and kept looking at his watch. Time passed so slowly. But finally, at three minutes after nine o'clock, he rang the Hansens' bell and marched slowly upstairs to her second-floor apartment. Sis was ready, and he was almost breathless when he saw her at the door, wearing a gold band about her hair and a semiformal dress, gold in color. Her arms were bare and plump, and he wanted to touch them.

She led him into the parlor. He quickly took off his glasses and put them in the breast pocket of his suit coat. He might seem more attractive without glasses. Maybe it had been these which had been responsible for his past failures with girls.

"But where's your glasses, Danny?"

"Oh, I took them off," he said self-consciously and unconvincingly. "It's good to give my eyes a little rest from them now and then . . . It's good for my eyes."

"Will any of the girls at the dance be wearing formal dresses?"

"Why, say, Sis, you look like a million dollars," he answered quickly, believing that he had said something appropriate that would impress her.

"But I want to know," she said with a touch of petulance, "if I'm wearing the right kind of a dress. Are you sure that none of the girls are going formal?"

"You look like a million dollars, Sis."

She looked at him, annoyed. He became awkward. He suggested that he call a cab and that they leave. He called the Yellow Cab Company from her telephone by the front door. Then he returned to the parlor and waited—silent, shy, and nervous. When they danced, he'd make a better impression.

The painful wait for the cab was brief, and they left. The cab went up to Garfield Boulevard and then turned into Washington Park. He sat on one side and she on the other. He wanted to sit closer to her but he didn't dare. He wished that they had already arrived at the dance. Then he'd show more life. He'd find his tongue.

"It's a swell night," he said, looking out at the big Washington Park ball field in the moonlight. He never played baseball any more.

"Yes," she said, uninterested.

"The dance is sure to go over," he said a moment later.

"Fine."

"My class is, on the whole, pretty good. But some of the guys in it are dumb."

She glanced out the window and didn't answer.

Had he said the wrong thing? What should he say? He didn't want to talk. He wanted to sit near her and feel close to her. He caught a whiff of her perfume, and he had a strong yearning to kiss her.

The cab passed out of Washington Park and bumped along East Fifty-fifth Street. Danny sat on one side, silent, with Sis on the other, looking out the window.

Walking through the lobby of the Warwick Hotel, Danny held his shoulders straight. He wanted to be seen now. They were early, and few of the dancers had arrived. He checked Sis's wrap and waited for her in the lobby while she went to the ladies' room. His eyes watered, and he wiped them with a handkerchief. But he looked better without his glasses. He'd try to get along without them.

The orchestra played a soft tune that he didn't recognize. He was eager to be dancing with Sis. Little Smilga came up and said hello. He hoped Smilga had seen his date. Smilga asked if he'd broken his glasses. He said that he hadn't and was keeping them in his pocket to give his eyes a rest. Bart Daly waved to him. He returned the greeting with a nod. Shanley, tall and callow-looking, passed, escorting a swell, dark-haired, simple-looking girl. He felt superior to Shanley.

He saw Sis walking toward him, and almost choked with pride. Yes, he told himself, he was in love with Sis. Danny went to meet her and suggested that they dance. They moved into the ballroom. There were only a few couples on the floor. She followed him well.

"It's like dancing almost with air, dancing with you, Sis," he said.

No reaction showed on her beautiful, expressionless face. She said nothing, but continued to follow him perfectly as he fox-trotted rapidly and then whirled her around in a corner. He wanted to talk, but there was a tense clamp of silence upon him. Now he had his chance for love, but he didn't know what to do with it. He didn't know what to say to her.

They danced as well as any couple on the floor. He glanced down at her face several times. There was no gleam of interest on it. The dance ended. He and Sis walked off the floor. He wanted to take her arm but didn't. More couples had arrived, and he nodded to classmates, proud of Sis's beauty but already beginning to feel desperate.

He met Marty Mulligan in the lobby and introduced Sis. Marty's smile told Danny that Sis had made an impression.

"The dance is going over," Marty said.

"Yeah, it's a big success. We did it," Danny responded eagerly, glad to have a subject of conversation and hopeful that Sis would be impressed.

"It's a good dance," Sis said listlessly.

Others joined them and they talked. Danny covered his nervousness with a beaming smile. His eyes ached, but he wouldn't put on his glasses.

The music started again. He led Sis onto the dance floor. Again they danced well together, but scarcely talked. Danny sensed that Sis was bored. He didn't know what to do, and began to wish that the dance were over and that he were riding home with her in a cab. She might let him kiss her. He wanted to kiss her.

Danny and Marty both hated Hal Clifford. He was plump and pouty-faced and was always trying to cadge money from fellows around Sixty-third and Stony Island and at Louisa Nolan's Dancing School where he hung out. He wasn't an S.S. student and had come to the dance as a stag, without having paid for a ticket. He joined the group and was introduced to Sis.

"Where have I met you before?" he asked her in a confident manner.

"Oh, you never can tell," Sis answered.

Danny knew that he had lost. The tone of Sis's voice had changed. The look in her eyes told him that Sis would go for Hal.

"You know, you're a paradox," Hal told Sis.

"Why?" Sis asked. "What does that mean?"

Bitterly, Danny thought that Sis was dumb.

"Yes, you're a paradox—familiar and rare," Hal went on.

"Yes?" Sis asked, openly flirtatious.

Angry, Danny saw them looking into each other's eyes. He wanted to bust Hal.

"Yes, your face is one of the rarest of faces, and yet it is as familiar as the day."

"You're kidding me now," Sis told him.

"I never kid," Hal said, speaking as though he were playing a well-rehearsed role.

Danny knew that Hal was a louse, and a dead beat as well. But Sis was falling for him. His anger turned to despair and a feeling of impotence.

The music for another dance started.

Hal stepped forward as though to lead Sis onto the dance floor without bothering to ask Danny's permission for the dance. Danny took Sis's arm, turned his back on Hal, and led her to the dance floor, his mood one of sullen determination.

"When I go to a dance, I don't always like to dance only with the same fellow," Sis said.

He restrained himself and did not tell her what he thought of Hal.

"Variety is the spice of life," Sis said.

"He didn't even ask my permission, and I am your escort," Danny told her. She said nothing.

But Danny knew now that he had failed. He had not made any impression on Sis. His eyes ached because he had gone without his glasses, and finally he put them on. Sis smiled at him coldly as he did this.

Danny exchanged dances with Marty and Hugh Mc-Neill, and for the rest, he fox-trotted silently with Sis, hoping for the night to end. When Hal did ask for a dance, he curtly turned him down.

His moods kept switching between panic, shame, agony, desperation, and futility. After the dance, the bunch went to the Bamboo Inn. He did not have a good time there either. Sis scarcely spoke to him. He still didn't know what to say to her. He laughed insincerely when Ike

Dugan and the others joked. He wanted to be alone with Sis in a cab. Perhaps then she would change. But he hoped without confidence.

And finally it was over and he got into a cab on Sixty-third Street with Sis. He gave the driver her address. They sat at opposite ends of the back seat. He yearned to take her in his arms and to find confidence and a feeling of beauty from the touch of her lips. If he didn't try to kiss her, wouldn't she think him slow, a dope? He had to make the effort, but he was too bashful, too timid. And if he tried and failed, he'd feel, all over again, a deep sense of humiliation.

The ride was brief. The cab stopped in front of the building at Fifty-ninth Street and South Park Avenue. Danny paid the fare, helped Sis out and accompanied her to the entrance hall.

In the lower hallway, Sis rang the bell, turned to face him, and said as though by rote: "Thank you for a perfectly grand evening."

"Oh, that's all right," he said in confusion.

"Well . . . good night."

"When will I see you again?" he asked, desperately refusing to give up.

"You'll have to call me."

The buzzer sounded. He clumsily tried to take her in his arms and kiss her.

"Not that," she said, evading him.

"Aren't you going to kiss me good night?" he asked, tense. She smiled coldly and was gone.

Hurt and dazed, he watched her walking up the steps of the inner hallway. He stood for a moment, defeated. Then he walked out. His shoulders slumped and after one glance up at the darkened window of her parlor, he slowly trudged home.

What was the matter with him? What was wrong with him? He looked at the sky and the shrubbery of the park across the street, and he was just hurt with a sense of defeat. His dreams of Sis and of love were dust.

Success Story

Dan Hallowell had the appearance of a college athlete. He was about six feet one, handsome in a conventional way, neat, well-mannered, nonchalant, and bland. He coasted through his four years in a midwestern college. He was intelligent, but shallow; and he was casual, both about others and himself. He didn't take his studies or himself seriously. He would often disagree with others students in bull sessions by blandly remarking: "Ah, the world's full of half-assed people." And when he was praised for his charm, he would say: "Me, I'm just another half-assed loon."

His smile melted the hearts of many. He made a number of conquests, but always managed to avoid scenes and troubles. He wasn't, in fact, deeply moved by girls. Making love was one of the things you did. But his reputation as a glamour boy fed his vanity. He liked to talk about girls, but he would always do this deprecatingly. Usually he would insist that love was a game and that all the talk and pretensions of romance were merely part of that game. He would expand on this theme, and behind these words there would be a bitterness of feeling which he would mask in smiles and in his unfailing and imperturbable air of blandness.

However, he was not a big talker, and more often than not he would listen to others, only now and then interjecting cryptic remarks. He would find a means of using the words "half-assed" and "bullshit" on such occasions. If his bland cynicism angered anyone, he would calmly tell the irate person not to become angry, and with that boyish smile on his face he would make a remark such as: "Listen, I'm only as half-assed as the next guy, and

80

don't expect another half-assed boy like myself to be profound."

Dan wrote easily and won the praise of his English teachers. He published sophisticated stories in the campus literary magazine, and in these he always contrived to include witty conversations. This wit would poke fun at sentiments, especially those of love. He also was working on a novel which he showed to no one. His friends and several members of the English Department kept urging him to submit his stories to magazines for publication, but he would always pass off these suggestions by saying that there were enough half-assed stories published as it was, and that he didn't want to add to this output.

He drank regularly, but he had a great capacity and despite the quantities of alcohol he consumed, he would never get really drunk. After several drinks, he would become benignly silent, except to say occasionally to someone: "How you doin'?" After getting a response, he would say: "Alcohol is the best and worthiest subject of human endeavor."

Dan had many friends, and yet he was intimate with no one. He responded to almost all people with the same pronounced blandness and casualness. His manner with girls was scarcely different from his manner with his male friends. He got on easily with many types of people and was rarely alone. He would spend hours with bores, and a bore or an interesting and intelligent friend seemed the same to him. In fact, he took all people in much the same spirit and they were, to him, all pretty much alike. One of his favorite expressions was: "Everybody can slip on the same banana peel."

The contrast between what Dan Hallowell seemed to be in the eyes of the world and what he was like in his inner life was sharp and dramatic. He was in his own eyes lonely and hurt. He regarded all life as futile, and he feared that any effort he made would be frustrated. To him, life was joyless. He looked down on people as pitiful creatures who would one day be old, become ill, and die, and then putrefy. He was obsessed with a sense of death, and he thought of death as the doom of all feeling, and he would quietly reason with himself that inas-much as death awaited all men, there was neither point nor purpose to living. Everyone was half-assed because everyone had to die. The best way in which to meet this fate was with a nonchalant smile. He used to tell himself that he wanted to be nonchalant when he came to meet his death.

Dan was secretly afraid of people and he envied them. How could they plan their lives and give all their heart and effort to some activity or to some feeling when they were doomed? How could they care? How could lads he knew tear their hearts out with love for some girl who was, in the last analysis, pretty much like any other girl? How could friends of his burn their lives out with worry lest they fail to become successes? How and why would people go on living?

Frequently when he was with people, he would think of them as pitiful, hopeless creatures who refused to ac-cept and meet the plain facts which predicted their doom. And he would interpret this by explaining to himself that there were few people who believed in the Ideal. He wanted to believe in the Ideal, but he considered himself too intelligent to accept any belief that would be betrayed. And he would then conclude that the basic betrayal of a human being was to be found in the fact that he had been born. Also, he would look at girls, and his eyes would travel up and down their figures, and then he would focus on their abdominal regions, and he would think to himself that there, there was the locus of the betrayal of all men, of all human beings. These reflections would fill him with disgust. And in the presence of women he would also think about menstruation, and this would intensify his disgust.

Sometimes in such moods, he would remember his boyhood. He had been especially happy during the period when he was eight to ten years old, and he would recall many scenes and episodes of that time. On rainy days he had stayed in the house and played with his electric trains, sometimes alone and sometimes with playmates. He would fancy himself an engineer, and he would dream end-lessly and find himself soothed by the noise of the train circling and circling the tracks. His father would be away at the office, and the presence of his mother would give him great comfort and security. And then there had been the animal pleasures of running and playing ball and climbing the old oak tree in the back yard. He would try to recapture a sense of those feelings, but he never could to his full satisfaction. And he knew that it was childish and irrational to want to be a little boy again, yet he did want just this, and again and again he found himself wishing that he were, once more, eight or nine or ten years old. How long the days had been! How sunny! How easy it had been to laugh! How he had wakened morning after morning thoughtlessly overjoyed with a sense of play and fun and mischief! How all life had seemed so warm and good and secure! And how he had never even dreamed or imagined that one could ever feel differently!

And yet even these memories had left him with feelings of bitterness. He had been living in a sunny dream that was unreal. He had been protected from reality and from a sense of death. He had found a joy that could not last, and he had wanted it to last. And knowing all this, he simply did not care and almost proudly assured himself that there was nothing that could ever make him care. It did not matter what you did, how you felt, what you wanted—everything meant the same thing: everything meant nothing. There were no values; all values were false, deceptive; they were traps and lures to deceive human beings.

Dan liked to fancy himself a philosopher, although he had no patience with formal philosophy. And what he considered to be his own disillusioned philosophy gave him pride and at times the conceit that he was highly sophisticated. He admired the Greeks. To him they were children of the mind. The early Americans believed that it was worth while to build a continent and to work with might and main to become a success in life. There was something of this American faith in his father, and he pitied his father. The old man had been born on a farm, had worked his way through a state university, had started with nothing, and had become a successful lawyer, up to his ears in deals, negotiations, contracts and civil suits. For years Dan had seen his father pore over papers, working on them night after night, worrying over them, and about the pocketbooks and the consciences of his clients. The old man had money. The family had all that it needed. His mother lived in boredom, comfort and nervous irritation. She had nothing to worry about, and that worried her most of the time. He couldn't figure out what was between his father and mother, and there was nothing between him and either of them. Because it didn't matter to him what he became in life, he accepted the idea of his father's that, after he graduated from college, he would go on to Harvard and get a law degree. The old man wanted him to be cultured, because he had never had any time for culture himself; he was fond of saying that the age of the self-made man was over and that the successes of the future would be men of culture and broad education.

Dan's father was absorbed in his own work, but as a way of escape. He felt secure in the courtroom, or behind his desk, or talking with a client in his capacity as a lawyer, or discussing aspects of the law with fellow lawyers, or when he buried himself in papers, reports, and briefs. His entire personality had been channeled and buried in his career and in his work, and his human feelings flowed through him like an undiscovered underground stream, known only by its echoes. For years he had scarcely uttered an intimate or humanly meaningful word to his son except by accident. He had allowed his own feelings to become lost in legal formulas because he was afraid of these feelings. He explained himself to his family, to others, and even partly to himself, by speaking constantly on the pressure of work.

In his youth he had struggled too hard, and he had concentrated his feelings and aspirations in his work with too much intensity for him to be able to relax. Success had cost him his feelings and the enjoyment. He had won himself a place in the world, but he was not sure of that place, and he was afraid to let up. He didn't know what he wanted out of life other than a continuance of what he already had, and he wanted this for its own sake. He was secretly troubled by a sense of inadequacy and limitation, but usually explained to himself that this was the price he had to pay for his position in the world. His ambition was to be appointed a judge. He was colorless as a human being, formal, friendly in a distant and insincere way, and, despite his successful practice, he did not make a strong impression on others.

Twice his name had been considered for judgeships, but on each occasion the appointment had gone to others. Sooner or later he would inevitably get his appointment, and he sometimes believed that when he did, he could relax the pressure he put on himself and that the security of his position would help him to feel that his place in the world was safe. And although he only occasionally thought of death, he was fearful of it. Whenever he drew up wills for clients, a vague and pessimistic mood would come over him. He would experience difficulties in talking of anything other than details of his work that were immediately in his mind, and he would weakly ask himself whether or not others felt about death as he did. He was cynical about human beings and regarded all idealism as impractical. Generosity was utopian and senseless. It was, he granted, unfortunate that there were rich and poor, but this was the way of the world. Weakness, failure, illness—all of these were part of a natural order of things, and an individual man could only try to avoid them. And interpreting the law according to your own interest and that of your clients was a mere act of self-protection. Success and the struggle for success were, likewise, means of self-protection. This was the kind of father Dan had.

When Dan was a college student, his father was a slim, medium-sized man with graying hair and spectacles, a man who dressed neatly and conservatively, walked with his head held rather rigidly, and concerned himself with his own affairs. He provided his family with comfort but little else.

Dan's mother had been the daughter of a grocery store owner. She had met Dan's father in college. Their romance had been proper, and they had married a year after their engagement had been announced. Her appeal to Mr. Hallowell had been connected with her meekness and her sense of social responsibility. She was not the kind of girl who would ever get herself talked about for her unconventional behavior. She was pliant and shy. Her shyness and youth were very appealing to him in those first days. And as he came to know her better, he realized that she was the kind of girl who could be relied on not to cause him worry or trouble when he was working hard and could not give her the time and attention many girls would want. He had married her because she seemed so suited to his nature, and he regarded her as the closest possible approximation to the ideal wife he was likely to find. From his standpoint she had served her function as wife. She had pliantly and obediently taken care of his needs, and she had done nothing to hinder him in the advancement of his career.

She was two years younger than Dan's father, and when Dan was in college she was a faded-looking little woman, with a few threads of gray in her hair and some wrinkles about her eyes. She was colorless and spoke in a low and spiritless voice, and experienced constant aches and pains. She ate sparsely, took many different kinds of pills, and was constantly shopping for new doctors because she could find no physician who could explain or cure her recurrent aches and pains, or help her to get over her chronic lack of energy. She went in for bridge, Baptist church affairs, and a ladies' literary society at which book club selections were discussed.

She was proud of Dan and afraid of him. Like her husband, she didn't know what to say to her son. She liked to wait on him; and she was secretly glad that he was taller, more athletic-looking than his father. She thought he was a good, decent, and pure boy.

Her evenness of temperament—or rather, her lack of temperament—had led Dan to think that she didn't love him. In his teens, he had sensed that the marriage of his parents was loveless, and in college he had picked up a smattering of Freudian ideas with which he interpreted his parents. They were repressed, he decided. He decided that he had never believed in the affection of his parents for him, or in their basic honesty. This discovery—for he regarded it as such—was gratifying. From it he drew the conviction that he had always been intelligent.

For Dan, life was usually dull. People were hollow, hollow men stuffed with insincerities. There was no conceivable activity into which one could throw oneself fully and completely. Life exposed surfaces behind which there was nothing. Life was like a scenic housefront with nothing behind it. He thought of many metaphors like this, and he enjoyed using them. And he saw all other questions as secondary. The emptiness of life was the prime question. And the answer to this question was clear and unmistakable.

Because he regarded life as empty, Dan believed that he was always looking at everything through the eyes of a blasé spectator. He was often quite conscious of himself, and he would have the illusion that he was two persons, one of whom watched the other and laughed and yawned and sneered while he looked on. He would even hold fanciful dialogues between the two persons who composed himself, and the one of him who was the spectator would compliment, condemn, and laugh at the other one. At times, when he would drink too much, he would gain the illusion that he had merged himself completely in the onlooker. Then he would imagine himself looking at the Dan Hallowell, whom the world knew, as cold and stonelike, dead.

Dan regretted graduating from college. He didn't want to go on to Harvard, and he discovered that he did not have a flair for law. However, the war postponed any decision; he was drafted. His personality served him well in the Army, and he did desk work all during the war. He was demobilized as a second lieutenant.

When he returned home from the Army, his father had become a judge. The man had relaxed somewhat and, with relaxation, he had begun to age. He looked old and tired. His hair was completely gray, and his face was beginning to wrinkle. With less to do, he became bored, restless and irascible. He wanted Dan to pick up where he had left off and to start right in at law school. Dan refused. There were sharp words between them. Dan taunted his father, declaring that he wouldn't have to spend a lifetime struggling to become a success. These words hurt Dan's father. The judge said no more, turning from his son and walking out of the room. And Dan had then stood alone, thinking that his revolt against his father had been easy, and had won him a hollow victory. He concluded that all victories were hollow.

Shortly after this scene, Dan picked up the manuscript of the novel he had worked on in college. He began by reading through it idly, but his interest picked up and his pride was roused. He decided that he would do the book over again and try to publish it. When he had contemptuously told his father that he himself wouldn't spend an entire lifetime in the struggle to become a success, he had not thought specifically of writing: in fact, he had not thought at all of what he might do with his life. Now he knew how he could win success and fame. He could write and become, perhaps, a rich and famous novelist. Why not? There were few living writers for whom he had any respect, and he considered himself to be equal to, if not the superior of, most writers in talent and intelligence.

Dan completed the revision of his novel in six months. It was conceived as the story of Dan's own generation in college and in war. The dialogue and the characters were modeled on the writings of Ernest Hemingway, but all sharp effects and all moments of keen feeling and sensibility were blunted by sophisticated witticisms. Suffering in the book was minimized. Life was both casualized and romanticized. The hero and his friends were presented as healthy, handsome, and Nordic, and the college girls were clever and somewhat glamorous.. The experience of war led them to settle down, and the conclusion of the novel emphasized the exact opposite of what Dan himself felt and believed. When his manuscript was completed, Dan smiled to himself and took pride in his own cleverness. He had a hunch that he would get the book published, and even imagined that it might be a best seller.

He planned to take the book to New York and to try to get some kind of job to support himself while he was trying to peddle it. He himself used the word "peddle." By accident he noticed an announcement of a ten thousand dollar prize-novel contest, and submitted his novel in it.

Dan won the prize. His book was also accepted by a book club. Critics hailed him as a genius and described him as the exponent of a new and healthy tendency in American literature. A motion picture company paid a six figure sum for the film rights to the book.

Dan Hallowell became rich, successful, and famous.

In the first months of his success, fame and money became a burden and a distraction to Dan. He was treated as a person of almost extraordinary importance. Having written one book, he became overnight a young man whose most passing and trivial remarks and witticisms were laughed at, valued, and quoted in gossip columns. If he took a woman to a night club, this was news. And he had so much money that it became valueless to him.

Dan enjoyed his fame and all these fruits of success as long as he was with people. But when he was alone, he poured contempt on those who flattered and praised him. His contempt was also turned on himself. He used the word "half-assed" more than ever and found himself growing increasingly resentful.

After nine months of the life of a celebrity, he became afflicted with ennui. He had two love affairs, but could feel no deep emotions for women. He seduced women with his tongue in his cheek and an unmoved heart. He regarded his book in the same light as he did the women he slept with. His own ecstasies were partly simulated, and behind them he would remain cold and objective. He could not believe that his women felt as passionate as they seemed to, and he would often imagine that they were deceiving him and, perhaps, also themselves. He looked upon his fame as something artificial, and at times he interpreted it as a means whereby people made themselves seem more important than they were. He had entered a world of celebrities where people like himself were needed in order that other people could involve their social lives, their pleasures, their amours and philanderings with a sense of achievement and significance. He was famous, he decided, as an excuse to justify the emptiness and the avarice of these people. And he prided himself on his in-

telligence in being able to see so clearly and in not letting
himself be taken in.

Success and fame, then, resulted in no important
changes in Dan Hallowell's attitudes or in what he styled
to be his philosophical outlook on man and life. He was,
on the whole, singularly unimpressed with his success in
all ways, save in the fact that he had proven how clever
he was and how he could be a success with such relatively
little effort.

Time passed and he did little work on his second new
book. Slowly and gradually this began to affect him. His
vanity became involved. Even though he periodically
thought that his success was not as great as his admirers
and flatterers made it out to be, he started to worry about
the possibility of failing because, were he to fail now, he
would be reduced to insignificance and he would be
laughed at and ignored. His distrust of and his contempt
for people served to deepen his worry because, if he failed
now, he feared that people would regard him as he now
regarded them. Only by being a success could he continue this game of fooling people, of showing up the world,
and of exhibiting his superiority. He saw himself as playing a phony role. And to fail would create the danger of
his being unmasked.

But he found himself with nothing to write about. He
made several attempts to start a new novel, but he char-
acterized these as half-assed drooling. He took to drinking
more heavily than he had ever done and he chased women
almost pathologically. He became particularly interested
in married women because they seemed to be safer as
conquests. The question of money began to prey on his
mind. A short while before he had placed almost no value
in it. Now he began to overvalue it. He didn't want to
spend it. He resented especially spending money on others
and, most especially, on women. Not only did people want
to ruin him with praise, but they also desired to take whatever he had away from him. They stole his time and
strength and energy and imagination. They were phonies.
They had turned him into a living symbol of phoniness.
Now, if he didn't come through again, they would scorn
him as a fraud. He continued to see people, to go to

parties and gatherings, and to chase married women, but
he did it resentfully. And he also began to complain about
the demands the phonies made on him. His hatred of
people became more active, more malignant, more viru-
lent than it had been in the past.

He turned down his third offer to work for a motion
picture studio, and in conversation with friends and acquaintances he told of this refusal in such a way that his
actions would be interpreted as a brave manifestation of
his integrity and his devotion to art. But he didn't need
the money, and he feared going to work in a studio on
the Coast lest he should fail as a scenarist. He had destroyed his own confidence with an obsessive fear of
failure. He began to talk in perfectionist terms and to de-
clare that he'd write no more half-assed novels. Now he
would work very patiently, and he would produce a book
that at least approached perfection. His friends told him
he was too modest; they tried to assure him that he had
already written a perfect novel, and praised him because
of the high literary ideals which he represented. He slyly
coaxed them on to praise him the more, to discuss his
work, his plans and his ideals, and at the same time he
suspected them because they did this. They were damned
fools!

Dan's way of life became increasingly empty. His sense
of this emptiness became all-pervasive. It filled his waking
hours. Morning after morning he sat down at his desk and
tried to work on a new novel. On some days he filled
pages and would even have some confidence in what he
produced. But this confidence did not last long, and he
would abandon what he'd written, only to begin all over
again. And on other mornings he would be unable to
write. Intense anxieties would seize him. He would become emotionally and intellectually paralyzed.

Six months of failure passed. His money began to dwin-
dle. He had published nothing in two and a half years.
Others had taken his place as new fair-haired boys of literature. His name was mentioned less and less in print.
People spoke less frequently of his work and of the novel
that he was presumed to be writing. He observed this, and
he led conversations around to the point where he could

talk of himself and explain why he was so slow in finishing his second novel. His glamour was worn thin, and he knew it. He drank more and more. He would wake up in the morning depressed, shaky, and he'd drink coffee and take Benzedrine pills. With this stimulus, he would try to write. He couldn't. One morning he told himself in disgust that he could write no more. He went out and got drunk. That was the day before he committed suicide.

When Dan's body was found in his gas-filled apartment, a ream of white typewriter paper was neatly stacked on his desk. The first page read:

A Success Story
by
Dan Hallowell

The second page read:

Dedicated to my parents

All the other pages were blank.

Norman Allen

One spring afternoon many years ago I came out of the university bookstore and encountered a group of friends. There were about eight of us. We chatted for a while and then went our various ways. This scene returns to me in memory because Norman Allen was one of that group.

Tall and brown-skinned, Norman always dressed neatly in the latest style. He liked light-gray suits and bright ties. Norman had high cheekbones, a lean face, restless brown eyes, and lips that were just a bit thick. You might be talking with him about a problem of philosophy or about the weather, and a meaningless smile would cross his face. He used to smile with no reference to what was being said and when nothing in a conversation called for it. His was a cold, impersonal smile that came and went like a shadow. It would distract and mildly disconcert you, and you would wonder why he smiled that way. What was the joke? You didn't get it. But then you would forget this and go on talking or listening to him. But again the disconcerting smile would flicker on his brown face. We sometimes discussed Norman, but I do not recall anyone ever speaking of his smile. Now across the years that separate me from youth and the days when I first knew him, that smile comes back to mind and remains fixed in my memory as one of his most significant traits. It was in a way more important than almost anything I recall having heard him say.

But I want to dwell for a moment on that casual scene of a sunny afternoon in May, over twenty-five years ago. Even though those were the days of the Depression, the future seemed open to us. Economic prospects were bleak, but in our group we did not talk and think merely of the

Depression. We expected to go on pursuing our intellectual interests. All of us had either intellectual or artistic
ambitions. The future seemed like an adventure in art,
ideas and living. We were what is perhaps best character-
ized by the phrase "liberal-minded." In our group Norman
seemed to feel at ease. He interested us because of his
intelligence and his brilliant promise in philosophy, and
not because he was a Negro. He was a protégé of Dr.
Dwight of the Philosophy Department; he had studied
under Whitehead at Harvard, and was an ardent admirer
of Dewey and Mead. He had a fellowship in the graduate
school and was working on his doctoral thesis. Big things
were expected of him.

On that particular afternoon, we talked for only a few
minutes. There was then a plan afoot for the publication
of a magazine to which both white and colored students
and Chicago young people would contribute. The pros-
pective editor was a jolly but erratic young colored man
named Dennison who had graduated and who bragged of
knowing Jack Johnson, former heavyweight champion of
the world. He claimed he was writing a biography of
Johnson, but the book has never been published and was
probably never finished. Dennison asked us all to contribute to the proposed magazine.

"We'll have Jack Johnson, philosophy, and advance-
guard aesthetics," he said with a laugh.

"Good," Norman said. "I'll write an article on Whitehead and the Negro problem."

I was not the only one who was struck by the apparent
inappropriateness of this remark. I remember that Carter,
who was considered a very brilliant student, laughed at it
when he and I were talking later.

"Allen is also making remarks like that," Carter observed. Anyway, Dennison promised to accept and feature
Norman's proposed article in the first issue. A few moments later I left the hatless group of young men and went
to Harper Library.

One afternoon shortly after this, I ran into Norman
and we walked to the campus together and then eastward
along Fifty-seventh Street. I did most of the talking. During this period I planned to write articles of literary

criticism from the standpoint of philosophy. I held then that you cannot only and solely interpret literature from the standpoint of itself, but that you need to bring ideas to bear on works of literature in order to render them more understandable. Norman was or at least seemed to be quite interested in my remarks.

"It's wonderful to look forward to writing like that," he said.

My talk clearly implied a faith about the future. And as I spoke eagerly and with enthusiasm, I assumed that Norman felt as I did.

Today this casual meeting takes on more meaning than it had at the time. The students strolling about, the coeds in their colorful spring dresses, the sight of so many young people, gave the scene an almost poetic freshness. On the campus was the possibility of learning and joy, and young minds and hearts could fill with hope, eagerness, a sense of the wonder of life and rich promises of tomorrow. The University and its campus was an island, green and quiet, amidst the tragic turbulence that was Chicago. And for a while Norman and I were youths who could be on that campus. Ideas and truths could be more important to us than anything else in the world.

We talked amiably and seriously as we walked. "Yes, how fine it is," he said, "to know what you are going to do in the future."

His remark, made a second time, seemed a bit singular to me. I believed that he also knew what he wanted to do with his life and where he expected to go. But my surprise quickly vanished. We continued talking about literature and philosophy for several blocks and then parted.

Norman worked as a janitor. He had little money and the circumstances of his life were hard, harder than I then realized. Later I was told of an incident in his life by Pete, a Greek studying at the University who knew Norman very well. Norman had told his friends that he was going to live at the home of a professor and give up his job as a janitor, although he would perform a few chores around the professor's home. His friends were all pleased to hear this news. It meant that he would be more comfortable and would have more time for study. And it seemed like a welcome example of the absence of race prejudice on the part of the professor. But one evening Pete visited Norman at the professor's home on Kimbark Avenue. Pete said Norman took him through the basement entrance and led him to a part of the basement close to the furnace. There was a dim electric bulb overhead, a small cot set very near the furnace, a scarred old dresser, and a few shelves on the wall for books. This was where Norman lived and sometimes wrote or studied. Pete had been shocked. He also said that Norman had been embarrassed.

Norman was exceptionally well-read for his age. He was then, in 1930, only twenty. But he was already firmly grounded in philosophy. He had been influenced by Nietzsche as well as by Dewey, Mead, Dr. Dwight, and Whitehead. He knew the thought of Hegel and Kant, and had also read the Greeks. In addition he was more informed, more interested in, and more sensitive to literature than most of the graduate students I knew at the University. And among the writers he had read and admired were Dostoevsky, Joyce, Proust, Thomas Mann, and T. S. Eliot. His reputation for brillance was rapidly spreading about the campus, and many already considered him a genius.

There was a little theater, the Diagonal, located at Fifty-seventh and Stony Island near the University campus. Pete had founded it and was its maestro. One of the students, Joan, a plump, handsome, black-haired girl with shining dark eyes, directed plays there. Joan was intelligent and kind as well as attractive. She put on a series of one-act Negro plays. These were well acted by an all-Negro cast and received much publicity in the Chicago press. Norman went around with the young Negro actors and actresses, most of whom were students. One of the group was his cousin, Sarah, an extraordinarily beautiful girl with lovely light-brown skin. Another of the group was Madeline, to whom Norman was engaged. She was a small, quiet, friendly, and extremely pretty girl with a light-brown skin. She and Norman made an attractive couple. Everybody thought that they were very happy.

When the Negro plays were put on, a number of parties

were held. At one of them Norman met Joan and fell in
love with her on sight. You could tell that he was in love
with her even though no one ever mentioned it, for whenever he saw her he would become intense and nervous as
he stared and gaped like a schoolboy. At times he would
seem to try and consume her with his eyes. He would be
unaware of and blind to everyone else, and Joan's presence
rendered him uncommunicative. And just as Norman was
attracted to Joan, similarly some of the white young men
were entranced by the colored girls, especially by Sarah
and Madeline. There was mixed dancing and some flirting,
but nothing more serious than this happened, even though
most of the group were free-loving Bohemians.

Insofar as anyone could observe, Norman's infatuation
for Joan did not cause any friction in his relationship with
Madeline. Charming and poised, she seemed sure of herself. Norman was attentive to her. Their devotion and
sweetness to one another were frequently commented
upon. But once he saw Joan, Norman ignored Madeline
and everyone else.

While very sympathetic to Norman, Joan was firm in
her refusal to have a love affair with him, and she told
him this as gently as she could. He became disturbed and,
at times, disconsolate. He would take long walks alone and
late at night, tramping and prowling the streets of the
South Side until dawn. And in a number of small ways,
his conduct became unpredictable. He stalked silently out
of groups for no apparent reason, and made remarks that
seemed strange or odd because of their irrelevancy.

For a number of months after the summer of 1930, I
did not see him. Then I left Chicago. However, I heard
that he had completed his doctoral thesis, received his
degree, married Madeline, been appointed to a faculty
post in the Department of Philosophy of a Negro university, and was launched on a promising career. I believed that he was happy and that he would go on to do
important work in his field. Once or twice when I met
mutual friends, I inquired about Norman and was told
that he was getting on well, and also that Madeline had
given birth to a son.

It seemed as though Norman were moving forward to a

productive and brilliant future and would have a happy personal life.

One day in New York a couple of years later, I met a friend from Chicago who told me that Norman had had a nervous breakdown and was recuperating in a private sanitarium. Then about three months later, I learned that he had been released and was again teaching. Six months after this I heard that he had been placed in a government mental hospital, but I was unable to get any information about his condition.

In 1935 I was in Washington. Carter, who worked there, had seen Norman, knew something of his illness, and told me he was in bad shape. Late one night just before he had been committed, Norman had gone out on the street wearing a top hat but, for the rest, stark naked. Carter also said that when Norman had been examined by psychiatrists he had been brilliant. Carter had visited Norman several times at the hospital, but then had stopped going because Norman wouldn't talk to him. It was pointless to see Norman, and Carter added that the poor fellow was gone.

From time to time after this meeting I heard chance bits of news about Allen. In 1937, for instance, Joan told me that Norman had been given insulin shock treatment and that there was hope that he would even be cured and released from the hospital. I read a few news stories about insulin shock treatment, and I believed that a cure for insanity had been found and that Norman and many others like him would be restored to society. The news pleased me. While I had never been an intimate friend of Norman's, I liked him and wanted him to do well in life, especially since he was colored. Now and then in the old days in Chicago, I had passingly thought and imagined that Norman would, by his expected success, help to disprove notions and biased claims about the lack of capacity for abstract thought on the part of Negroes. But Norman did not recover. More years went by. Occasionally I still heard that Norman was in the hospital, and that there had been no change in his condition.

In 1945, accompanied by two doctors in residency at the hospital, I visited Norman. He was a patient of Dr. Strauss, who was young, thin and bespectacled and in his second year as a resident psychiatrist. The other doctor, Dr. Arnold, was also young, but was on another service at the hospital.

It was the end of a June day, and the sun had begun to sink as we drove to the ward building. The hospital grounds were large and attractive, and they had the aspect of a campus. In the automobile Dr. Arnold said: "Allen has become what's called a backward patient."

"Has he ever been your patient, Doctor?" I asked.

"No, but Abe Strauss here is his doctor. I've heard Allen discussed a lot around here and I know that a fortune has been spent trying to cure him."

"Who spent it?" I asked.

"Foundations and universities."

"He's been examined," Dr. Strauss said, "by a number of the most able and important psychiatrists in America." He then mentioned the names of several famous or well-known psychiatrists who had been brought in on Norman's case.

"What happened?" I asked.

"Nothing," Dr. Strauss answered. "Nothing has helped."

"Isn't there any hope for him?" I asked.

"The prognosis is poor," Dr. Strauss said.

"Wouldn't electric shock treatment help him?"

"No, I don't think so."

"What's wrong with him exactly?" I asked.

"He's a paranoid schizophrenic," Dr. Strauss answered.

We parked in front of the ward building. It was old and of a dull red brick. Seeing it in the fading light, I had an overpowering feeling of dreariness and hopelessness, and also of sordidness. I knew that this would be a sad experience. Getting out of the automobile, a state of awe came over me. I had already seen enough of this institution and of its inmates to be deeply touched and inexpressibly saddened by the spectacle of wholesale insanity. Unlike the doctors accompanying me, this was still new and unfamiliar. I had heard the wild, shrill, angry and frightened

screams and curses of the inmates echoing through the
pleasant green grounds. I had talked with some of these
patients. And now I was going to see Norman Allen and
he was one of them.

It had been years ago, in my youth, that I had last seen
him. We had talked about the ideas of Dewey and Whitehead and about the future. I recalled that once on campus
he had told me that, after receiving his degree, he planned
to teach. And I had said I would write literary criticism
and, somewhat shyly, that I was writing a novel. And the
novel that I had then been writing had made me somewhat
famous. And then, after many years, there was I, entering the dreary building where Norman was confined.

"He probably won't even recognize you or know you,"
Dr. Strauss told me as we walked toward the building
entrance.

I had the vain and excited hope that Norman would
recognize me, and the even more vain and naive hope that
somehow my visit would touch and move him and would
help him a little to recover.

The interior of the ward building was clean but dimly
lit. The walls of the corridor had been recently painted in
white and the waxed floors gleamed. Several inmates stood
in the first-floor corridor, along the walls or in front of
opened room doors.

"How are you?" Dr. Arnold asked one of the patients.
He was a big black man, and he had tied and wound
many old rags about his chest and shoulders. The inmate
mumbled something to Dr. Arnold that I did not catch.

"What do the voices say?" Dr. Arnold asked.

The inmate grinned foolishly.

"What are these for?" Dr. Arnold asked, pointing at the
old rags on him.

"To keep the voices out," the inmate answered.

I heard several wild shrieks—loud, piercing, not quite
human, throbbing with pain and violent with anger. We
continued along the corridor. Some of the inmates ignored
us; others stared.

We entered a large ward room on the right. Six inmates
were sitting or lying on the beds. A man in pajamas

howled. The five others paid no attention to him. On the
bed nearest the door lay a lean, brown-skinned man staring at the ceiling with fixed eyes. I recognized Norman
instantly.

But he was changed. He was thinner than he had been
fifteen or so years ago. His cheeks were hollow, giving
more prominence to his high cheek bones. And his eyes
were sunken and there were hollows around them. He wore
a nondescript pair of unpressed gray trousers and a white
shirt.

As we approached his bed he lay motionless; his eyes
were dull and glazed and there was a mad, absent look
in them. We stopped at the side of his bed. His eyes lit up
in surprise, came to life, and for a few seconds his face
lost its masklike rigidity.

Imagining that he had recognized me, I was flattered.
But if he had recognized me, I wouldn't have known it.
Who and what I was and represented in his distorted mind
will remain, along with many of his fears, secrets, hopes,
and thoughts, a mystery never to be unraveled.

"Hello, Norman," I said, speaking gently and softly. He
lay in a catatonic state, staring at the three of us.

A kinky-haired madman on the bed next to Norman's
let out a violent shriek. I told Norman my name, but he
did not respond; he fixed me with dull, glazed eyes.

"Do you remember me, Norman?" I asked.

Again the kinky-haired madman shrieked. He made
loud, angry cries, but none of the patients looked at him
or in any way revealed that they heard him. He was in
his forties and there were touches of gray in his tangled
black hair. He paused for a moment and then, as though
with a fresh energy, he yelled again. I saw through the
window behind him that it was twilight and when he again
paused, I heard the chirping of birds.

"Don't you remember me from Chicago, Norman? Do
you remember Joan? And Carter?" I still spoke softly and
gently. And he continued to fix me in a rigid stare.

Dr. Strauss called an attendant, who came to us quickly.
He was medium-sized and plump. Dr. Strauss instructed
him to give Norman an injection of sodium amythol.

The kinky-haired madman continued yelling. Dr.

Strauss told him to be quiet. Ignoring the doctor, he screamed with increased intensity and violence.

"He's always like that. Tell him to be quiet," said a patient sitting on a bed to my left. He was a young Negro with dark skin.

The madman howled. Dr. Strauss told me that he was from a very rich merchant family on one of the Caribbean islands. The attendant came back to our group carrying a needle, a bottle of alcohol, and a piece of cotton. As he leaned down to give the injection, rubbing Norman's arm with alcohol, Norman let out a low growl. Then he trembled as the attendant jabbed the needle in, but quickly he looked up with pained submissiveness.

In a few moments he said to me: "I know you." However, his face did not become very expressive. He rolled his eyes and pointed to Dr. Arnold whom he had never seen before.

"But I don't know you. You're not in the picture." Then he pointed to Dr. Strauss. "I know you."

"Norman, remember . . ." I began. The kinky-haired madman shrieked. "Do you remember me, Norman?" I asked. The kinky-haired madman shrieked again.

Norman rolled his eyes, glanced at the howling inmate, and smiled briefly in pleasure. He turned toward me, and I saw on his face the same smile I had seen years ago on the University campus.

"He's in trouble," Norman said, referring to the howling madman.

"How are you, Norman?" I asked, hoping that by speaking softly and gently I could reach him.

"Be quiet! I hear you," Dr. Strauss told the madman. He quieted down. Dr. Strauss spoke with Dr. Arnold and the attendant about taking Norman to a room where it would be easier and more convenient to talk with him. The attendant said that there was a vacant room down the corridor.

"Come, Allen, we'll have a talk," Dr. Strauss said. Norman allowed the attendant to help him get off the bed. He walked at a careless, shuffling gait as we left the ward room.

In the corridor the inmate with rags bound about his

chest greeted us with foolish grins. Behind me I heard babbling talk. Norman shuffled at my side with his eyes on the floor. His shoulders drooped.

We used a small room. Norman sat facing us, with his back to the open window. The hospital bed was on his left. Through the open window I could see a hedge of rich green bushes, and their fragrance floated in through the open window. The persistent song of insects, the natural perfume of the shrubbery, and the thickening blue sky, all spoke to me of another world than this small one of mania. Norman could not walk alone by those bushes, nor could he stand alone under that sky. Did he ever yearn to or want to, or was the open sky another of the terrors that made him shiver with fear? Did that blue open sky symbolize a freedom too terrifying for him even to contemplate?

After we were seated, I took out a package of cigarettes.

"Give me one," Norman said.

I offered him an opened pack. He pulled out a cigarette and immediately tore it to bits which he let drop in an ash tray. Then he ground and squashed the tobacco and played with it as a small child might.

He stared at me as though I might be a meaningless object. Sitting there a few feet away from me, he could have killed me, and not for anything I had done or would do to him, but rather because of his own fears. And these were no different from the fears that could terrify and destroy us all, were they to rage unchecked in our nature as they must have in Norman's.

He was not quite human. He was a shell with all the form that humans possess. My regret, my sadness, my awe was deep. And I felt about him something of what I should have felt about myself had I been so stupidly and stupefyingly drunk as to have destroyed all consciousness and self-control. I saw in him the most tragic of all kinds of waste, the waste of human emotion and thought.

I hoped Norman would talk sensibly. There, in that small room as twilight spread beyond the window, I hoped Norman would come back from his dream world.

"Don't you remember me, Norman? Don't you remember when we would sometimes talk?"

"I remember you," he answered flatly. "I met you at State and Madison. But him——" Norman pointed at Dr. Arnold, "——he's Himmler. I met him with Himmler at State and Adams. Himmler, Hitler."

"Allen, do you know that Hitler's dead?" Dr. Arnold asked him.

"Yes, the Fourth International killed him. It's June, 1953. The Fourth International killed him in Cuba."

This was very painful. But my feelings were also qualified by curiosity. I had seen madmen and madwomen on streets, and I had talked with some of them here at the mental hospital. But it had been different from sitting there with Norman and remembering him fifteen years before when he had been so different, and had been known as a brilliant student and possibly a genius.

"Do you know what year it is?" Dr. Strauss asked him.

"1945. My son is older now."

"Yes, that's true. It is 1945," Dr. Strauss said.

"There are houses out there," Norman said, pointing stiffly at the open window through which no houses were visible.

"What do you think about all day, Allen?" Dr. Strauss asked.

"I hear them."

"Do you hear voices?"

"White women. Their voices are very sweet. They talk to me like music. They talk to me. I compose symphonies . . ."

He reached for another cigarette, and I gave him one. Immediately he crushed it and played with it in the ash tray. He stared at me as though he had never seen me before.

"Do you remember Dr. Dwight?" I asked.

He laughed at me quietly and as though he had played a joke on me.

"Do you remember, Norman? Do you remember how we talked about Dr. Dwight's papers, and about Whitehead?"

He played with the broken cigarettes and the tobacco in the ash tray. He swept me with a haughty look.

"Allen, why did you play with your feces in the toilet bowl the other day?" Dr. Strauss asked.

"To find contentment in the womb," Norman answered with a suggestion of contemptuous laughter in his voice.

Norman seemed hopeless to me, but still I was not ready to give up. I wanted him to recognize me. I was convinced that he did, even though he would not say so. I wanted him suddenly to become more sane and rational, and I believed that he could if he would only take the step.

I looked out of the window at the fading twilight and I heard the insect chorus as something fresh, a call to feel and love the world and life. And the dark green bushes seemed so verdant. For a moment, I felt myself alone and set apart, and I listened to the chirping insects. It was like a call to and a celebration of some beautiful world which existed somewhere out there beyond the window and under that sky which was now a deep rich blue. Then I realized, as if anew, where I was. Again I saw Norman, the two doctors, and the hospital room—a small drab room with bare green walls, a hospital bed, simple chairs, a table, and a stand. It was the kind of room in which one could die alone.

I thought of how madmen must have been confined to this room and lain on that bed, and of how they must have screamed and shrieked in their traumatic fears, terrors, and angers, fighting unseen foes and assailants and filling their minds with strange and distorted dreams and visions.

I looked at Norman again. There was a shadow of coldness across his face, an unchanging stare in his eyes, and a smirking suggestion of a smile on his lips. I told myself what I knew—that Norman was mad, mad, unalterably and hopelessly mad. I tried to reach him with a friendly gaze. He met it with a chill and unrecognizing look. I smiled. His face did not change.

"Norman, don't you remember . . ." I began.

"I remember those houses," Norman interrupted in his flat voice.

"Where are the houses?" Dr. Arnold asked.

"Right out there beyond the window. You live in them."

"Don't you know, Allen, that there are no houses right out there beyond the window?" Dr. Arnold asked.

"I see them. It's May, 1945. Those houses, there they are."

"Do you know where you are, Allen?" Dr. Arnold asked.

Norman nodded affirmatively.

"Do you know what kind of place this is?" Dr. Arnold asked.

Norman grinned foolishly.

"What do the voices say?" Dr. Strauss asked after Norman had failed to answer Dr. Arnold's last question.

"They are sweet and soft."

"Why are you here?" Dr. Arnold asked.

"I am happy here. I like it."

Norman's talk became incoherent and disjointed. I did not pay close attention to it. I thought he had probably told the truth when he had said that he was happy in the hospital.

"The houses are green. Green houses. Carter. Marya Carter."

"Marya is Carter's wife," I interrupted. "Do you remember Carter at the University, Norman?"

"I met him at State and Madison with Himmler there." Norman looked at Dr. Arnold. "Hess wasn't there. I don't know Hess. I like it here. I am perfectly happy. The green houses aren't happy. I compose beautiful symphonies. White woman never slept with me."

"Why do you say that, Allen?" Dr. Arnold asked.

I leaned forward, eager to hear his reply. I could not help believing that he was better oriented in the present situation than would seem the case, judging from his conduct and his conversation.

"I don't like him," Norman said.

"Do you remember the University and Dr. Dwight, Norman?" I asked.

"Dr. Dwight. They don't sleep with me. They talk to me. Voices soft, sweet." He spoke as though everything he said were self-evident.

"Allen, why do you think white girls won't accept you?" Dr. Strauss asked.

Norman grinned at the doctor as though he were an idiot.

"There are men of your race who have married white women," Dr. Arnold said.

"They only talk to me. All day. I compose. They talk sweet."

"Why do you sit masturbating in the ward, Allen?" Dr. Strauss asked.

"For them, when they talk to me."

"What do they tell you?" asked Dr. Strauss.

"Life. There's life in the houses, life in the green houses. But they won't let me in."

"What houses, Norman?" I asked.

"Out there. Out-houses, green houses. They go there and sing to me."

"Allen, even if white women won't accept you or sleep with you," Dr. Arnold said, "is there any reason why you should be here? Do you know where you are?"

"In a comfortable place and they talk to me like songs. Sweet, soft music . . . Schumann."

"Don't you want to go out into the world again and teach?" Dr. Strauss asked.

"Outside, somewhere outside, I hear a wild cry, a shriek," Norman said.

"Why don't you talk more, Allen? Why do you lie in bed all day, silent?" Dr. Arnold said.

"I talk to myself. Yourself, myself, you're good company to myself. Voices like music, soft voices, speaking music."

"You don't have to be afraid to go out into the world, Allen," Dr. Arnold said. "You can make your own way and be a brilliant person."

A cold smile came over Norman's face.

"Norman, do you remember one day on campus when we talked of Whitehead?" I asked.

He looked at me with a face as close to being expressionless as a human face could be. "Hegel wrote the dialectic. Yes, no, no, no, no, no, no, Nora, nobody no white heads for me."

"You studied under Whitehead. Don't you remember, Norman? You wrote your doctoral thesis about his thought," I said.

"Bridgeheads to the moon, did you ever think of bridgeheads to the moon? The moon will come up. I can never build bridgeheads to the moon with Professor Bridgehead."

"Don't you know, Allen, that you aren't talking sense?" Dr. Arnold asked.

"On the moon, you have supersense, surrealism."

"Norman, you were a pragmatist in your thinking, I remember," I said.

"Allen, what is a pragmatist?" Dr. Strauss asked.

"Pragmatism is the ascertainment of meaning," Norman answered.

Struck by his ready definition, I said:

"And the pragmatic theory of knowledge, Norman, what is it?"

His eyes wandered vacantly about the room. His face did not change.

"What is the purpose of life, Norman?" I asked.

"To create the ideal inner self."

"Can you create it here, Allen?" Dr. Arnold asked.

"I'm going good. Good, better, best."

"Could you do better outside in the world, Allen? Is anything worse than being here in your condition?" Dr. Arnold asked.

"Doing good, better, west. Go west young man. The wester you go, the wester you are. Yes, I like it here."

The two doctors looked at one another knowingly.

"You won't get anything out of him," Dr. Arnold said.

Dr. Strauss nodded in agreement.

They both rose, and Dr. Strauss left the room. I looked at Norman, trying to think of something more to say, but my mind went blank. I felt deep sorrow. But I was still convinced that Norman knew more, recognized more and remembered more than he would admit or reveal to us.

The attendant entered the room, and Norman rose and docilely followed him into the corridor. Dr. Arnold and I followed.

"Good-by, Norman," I said.

He did not answer.

I watched him shuffle along the dimly lit corridor. An inmate in one of the rooms screamed. We left the building.

Driving away as it grew darker, Dr. Arnold said: "Yes, he's like a shell of a human being."

"I think he knows more than he will admit," I said.

"Possibly," Dr. Strauss said. "But there's no way of reaching him."

"He seems to me to be incurably sick," Dr. Arnold said.

We got out of the car in front of another building. I heard a woman screaming from behind a barred window. From other buildings the plaintive, shrieking chorus of mad men and women cut the spring night.

Two years after I had visited Norman, I heard that he had gouged out one of his eyes. Then, a year or two later, I learned that he had died of pneumonia.

Joe

Joe used to be our butcher. He worked in a busy shop on East Twenty-ninth Street, near Third Avenue, and we always used to ask for him to wait on us. He was an Italian-American, over six feet tall, slender, rather raw-boned, dark and handsome. Whenever we tried to talk with him about anything other than meat, he wouldn't have much to say. He seemed to be an omadhaun. Several times I framed careful questions, hoping to learn what he felt or thought or believed about politics, about Mussolini and about the invasion of Ethiopia. I got no answer. But he was a good butcher. He was completely methodical in his work. His salary was about twenty-five dollars a week.

When we first began to trade at this butcher shop, he would slip us bad pieces of meat, expensive cuts, tough steaks. Gradually when we got to know him, and since we kept coming there regularly and asked to have him wait on us, he began to take pains to find good cuts for us. He would give us advice about what meat to get, which saved us small sums. Sometimes, if it was raining, or we were too tired or busy to go out for meat, we would call up for it and speak to him over the phone. The meat would be delivered. If no one else was able to deliver it, Joe would come himself.

Several times when Joe delivered meat to us, we asked him if he wanted a drink. He didn't drink. He didn't smoke. We asked him if he were married, and he told us that he couldn't afford to support a wife. He lived at home with his old mother. When we got to know him a little better, he would usually talk about the weather, or he would offer advice on cooking roasts. If we asked him what he thought of President Roosevelt, he would shrug

110

his shoulders and say that he guessed he was all right, and doing the best that he could. If we asked him what he thought about Mussolini, he would shrug his shoulders and say that he guessed Mussolini was doing things for Italy. He was for the New York Giants in baseball, and he felt that the major league magnates had not given Babe Ruth a fair deal. Babe Ruth, he said, should have been made manager of the Yankees.

During a strike of elevator operators we asked Joe what he thought of it. He guessed that they weren't getting enough money to live on, he said.

"But I might be called out for it," Joe said.

We asked him what he meant.

"I'm in the police reserve," he said, with pride.

"No, I don't believe it," my wife answered.

"Yes, I went to the police training school. I might be called out any day now."

"Will you like that, Joe?"

"What do you mean?"

"Would you like it to have to go out and beat up strikers who are fighting for a few more dollars a week?"

"No, of course not."

"Would you hit strikers fighting for a decent living wage?"

"No, I wouldn't want to. Every man wants to get along, doesn't he?"

"Well, what'll you do then, if you are called out?"

"Well, I'll have to go."

"And then what will you do? Will you hit strikers?"

"Oh, I guess I'll have to do what I'm told to, won't I?"

"What do you want to be a policeman for, Joe?"

"There's more money in it. I can't make enough money here. If I want to get married, you know, or save a little something for a rainy day, well, I can't get it working here. I only make twenty-five dollars a week. I wouldn't mind being a butcher if I made more."

"Are you getting married?"

"Oh, no!"

"Haven't you got a girl?"

"Well, no, not now. But sometimes a man gets a girl, and he marries her. And I want to have a little saved up.

It's not that I want to be a policeman. But there's no future for me as a butcher. So I went to the police training school. I passed all my examinations, so I'm on the reserve now. I'll be put on sooner or later."

"Will you have a future on the police force?"

"Yes."

"How much of a future? Will you be able to be a sergeant some day?"

"No. I didn't go to high school. Not much chance of being a sergeant if you haven't been to high school."

"How much of a future will you have?"

"A steady job and higher wages. I'll make about a hundred and sixty a month."

"But what about having to beat up people. If you go out now, you'll have to beat up elevator operators, strikers who want fifteen and eighteen dollars a week for themselves, and for their wives and families."

"Of course, we all have to do things that we don't like to do. That's life."

"That's right. But you have this job, and even if it doesn't pay you as much, you won't have to be beating people up."

"I thought about that. But a man has to look out for himself, you know. Because if he doesn't, nobody else looks out for him. And then too, people should try and not break the law. I don't like people who break the law."

"Do you think the elevator strikers are breaking the law?"

"Well, yes and no."

"What do you mean?"

"A man has to do something to make a living, but they shouldn't break any windows or cause disruptions."

"Well, what'll you do if they call you out?"

"Me, I'll have to obey orders."

After that we used to ask Joe if he had been called onto the force yet. He would generally tell us that he expected to be called soon. About two months after the strike of the elevator operators he wasn't in the shop any more, and another butcher told us that Joe was now a policeman. After that we would sometimes ask for him when we went to buy meat. Nobody had seen him for several weeks—since he had gone on the force. Then one day, one of the other butchers told us that Joe had been around.

"How does he look in his uniform. I'll bet he's handsome," my wife said.

"He didn't wear it."

"What, was he off duty?"

"Yes, he didn't wear it."

Then again, we learned he had come around, and we asked about him, and about the kind of a cut he made in his policeman's uniform.

"Oh, Joe's not happy."

"What's the matter?"

"He doesn't like it. He's ashamed."

"Why?"

"He's ashamed to come around and show his uniform. He always wears other clothes when he comes here."

"Why is he ashamed?"

"Yes, he's ashamed. Joe's not happy on the force. But you can't blame him. He's a good fellow, and he doesn't like it, being a copper. Why some day he might have to pinch his own friends. Nobody can tell when a cop might have to arrest his own mother. No, Joe's not happy. He's ashamed of himself, and he's afraid to come and let his old friends see him in a stool pigeon's uniform. He's making good money now, but I don't envy him none. He's a good fellow too. But he's not happy now. No, he doesn't feel that he was cut out to be a stool pigeon, and Joe knows it. All his old friends hardly want to talk to him. No, lady, Joe isn't popular around here any more, like he was when he was behind this counter, wearing an apron."

Saturday Night in Paris

It was a warm and quiet Saturday night in June. A couple of girls were out early, plying their trade on the Rue Washington. There was a crowd on the Champs Elysées. Many sat in cafés. Others promenaded. Before several motion-picture houses there was a waiting line. The traffic was heavy.

Marie and I drove along to the Place de la Concorde. It was lit up and elegant, and many automobiles were passing through it. We turned left and found a place to park near the American Embassy. Two French blue-caped policemen stood on guard in front of the closed gate of the Embassy grounds. Nothing was happening. A French couple passed by not even noticing the policemen.

"I didn't expect any excitement," I told Marie. "But I thought that we might stop by and take a look."

"Yes," she said.

There had been a riot early that morning and I had read in the newspaper that some Algerians had been shot. The day before, the news had come that Julius and Ethel Rosenberg had been executed. Excitement had run high in Paris, and all over France for that matter, because of the Rosenberg case. The newspapers had printed much news and comment, and the greater portion of this reflected unfavorably on the United States. Resentment and feeling had spread far beyond the circles of those influenced by the French Communist Party. A large proportion of France seemed to think that the Rosenbergs should not be executed. Many regarded this as a new Dreyfus case. Americans had been insulted or treated coldly on the streets and in cafés and restaurants. I had observed this feeling on the part of waiters in cafés where I had gone.

114

And the Rosenbergs had been executed. It was a fine June night. Life was going on in Paris. The two policemen stood at the closed gates before the American Embassy, bored. One of them lit a cigarette.

We approached the two policemen and Marie asked them in French if there was anything happening. They said "no" rather casually. And they expected no rioting or trouble on this evening. There had been some trouble, not too much, on the night before. Marie nodded towards me and told them that they were guarding my property. I was an American, she said. The two French policemen did not comment.

We walked off.

Nearby and parked by a curb, there was a bus load of French police. Some sat in the big bus. A couple stood by the rear. We talked with them. They were young and pleasant. Marie asked them if they expected any rioting. One of them answered in the negative, speaking casually but with definite assurance. A second young policeman, who sported a moustache and was smoking, remarked that if the Communists caused any trouble, they would be handled. A third expressed regret that there was no riot and felt his club, almost affectionately. There was a twinkle in his eyes.

Marie spoke with the policemen for a few more minutes and told them that I was an American. We said good-bye. They politely said: "Bon soir, monsieur— 'dame."

We left, got back into the car, drove through the Place de la Concorde, crossed over to the Left Bank and went along the Boulevard St. Germain to the Place St. Germain. We were going to the Deux Magots.

The sidewalks were crowded, and in front of the Deux Magots, the cars were parked thickly. Across from it on the opposite side of the place, there was a police wagon. Policemen stood by it, idle, with nothing to do and no riots to quell.

Seeking a place to park in the parking area before the Deux Magots, I noticed a car starting to leave and quickly told Marie to drive into the spot it was vacating. Another car was backing into this same space from the opposite direction. We were stopped when we were about half way into this space. The driver of the other car did nothing. He blocked our passage.

"What am I to do?"

"Nothing," I answered.

We sat and waited. The other driver also did nothing.

"This place should be ours."

"Yes," Marie said.

We waited a moment, expecting the driver of the other car to back out. He didn't budge. He sat at his wheel, waiting, just as we were.

"Don't move," I told Marie.

We waited perhaps thirty seconds, perhaps a minute or even a minute and a half. Then, I recalled that the police were across the street, and at the same moment, Marie said: "Call the agent."

I got out of the car, dashed across the street and spoke to a young policeman. I began to speak in rather ungrammatical French and with a pronounced American accent. But I made myself understood and the young *flic* followed me across the street.

The driver of the other car got out in a rage. He was a medium-sized man and was wearing a brown tweed suit and a brown felt hat. He sported a handle-bar moustache. He spoke volubly and angrily. The young policeman looked at him and listened unimpressed by the man's angry words. Once or twice, the policeman nodded his head as the man with the handle-bar moustache demanded that he be given the parking space. A crowd collected. I stood near Marie trying to frame French sentences in advance so that I would not be at a loss for words when my turn to speak came.

The policeman nodded his head again and while the man with the handle-bar moustache still fumed, he turned to Marie.

She spoke quietly and reasonably. She was very pretty and gave the impression of being an unprotected woman.

The crowd of spectators increased. Some were silently curious, while others were talking and airing their opinions about the incident. I kept trying to frame French sentences and wanting to intervene, but Marie explained the situation quite satisfactorily and I got no chance to speak. The other driver fumed. He wanted to say more, and he barked out his protests and his rancor to several bystanders.

The young policeman nodded several times to Marie, told her to back out of the vacant position, and then gave the same instructions to the other driver. He was surly, but turned away, went to his car and got in. Two women and another man were in his automobile. He and Marie both complied with the policeman's order. Then, Marie was told to take the vacant parking place. She drove into the spot. The other driver found space by the curb near the Café des Deux Magots. The incident appeared to be closed. We locked Marie's car. The crowd was dispersing. The policeman stood watching, with folded arms.

The policeman began to walk back toward the van across the square, but the man with the moustache strode up to him and began shouting. He had found a place to park, but something was eating and rankling him. He talked fast, angrily and loudly, denouncing the policeman for having been unjust. It was all right not to have allowed him to park, if the blonde woman also had not been permitted to do it either. The policeman had said that neither of them should park and that they weren't entitled to the place. And then, there was the other car parked where it shouldn't be. He was going to turn the policeman in, and cause him trouble.

The policeman had listened coolly. When the fuming fellow kept on shouting and asked for his number, he asked for the man's papers. The man refused to give them.

By this time, three more *flics* had crossed the square to the scene of the argument. Unexpectedly and without warning, they grabbed the man and gave him the bum's rush across the street and into the van.

A number of the watching bystanders laughed. The party of three who had been in the man's car also crossed the street and entered the big police van.

A few of the bystanders talked and laughed, and Marie described what had happened. Then we found a table on the crowded café terrace.

"Goddamn fool," I remarked.

"Yes, he was idiot man," Marie said.

"I wonder what's eating him?"

"He was not gallant."

"More than that, he wasn't right."

"He was son of a bitch," Marie said. She had learned this phrase from me.

The waiter came and we ordered.

"Well," I said, "he spoiled his own Saturday night but not ours."

The newspaper coverage of the Rosenberg case had been giving an impression that Paris was electric with excitement. And there had been tension in the atmosphere. At my hotel, guests had spoken heatedly of the case. One woman, the wife of a Mexican, had spoken proudly of how all France was united. She seemed to be a vain and unserious woman, and, most certainly, she had no knowledge of the case. But now, sitting in the Deux Magots, Paris and life seemed normal and untroubled. The sidewalk was crowded, and people milled back and forth. A fair number of the faces were familiar to us because we had often gone there.

And all about us there was conversation, mostly in French. Now and then, we heard Americans talking. I would look to see if I knew the Americans. I had not been seeing many Americans, and sometimes I was lonesome to talk more with Americans. I felt so especially at this period because I knew from the press, and also in a smaller way from personal experience, that there was a wave of anti-Americanism in Paris. But I saw no Americans whom I knew.

I sat back and looked at the tower of the old abbey opposite me. It was there, set like something eternal and framed against a clear blue sky that also seemed eternal. The Romanesque tower, simple and sturdy, suggested the depths of time, time lost in the centuries which had slid away from man forever. The sky suggested the vast expanse of space, space that would be forever unconquerable by man. I looked at the crowd and thought with a certain sadness that it was all over and the Rosenbergs were *dead*. The finality of death awed me.

Marie had been sitting quietly and looking about.

"The police will beat that man up."

"How do you know they will?"

"They always do."

"Damned fool. He brought it all on himself."

"He was a rude man."

"There's Bernard."

A tall Frenchman in a gray suit walked by and was lost in the crowd to our right on the corner.

"This is his corner," I said, merely making conversation.

"He wants to be *chef de cabinet* in the Ministry."

"He has to be something," I said dryly.

I remembered early years when I had sat in this same café and looked at the tower of the abbey, and at French people. I had wondered and pondered about the French, idly and casually. When you do not know what the homes of people are like, what their ambitions are and other such matters concerning them and their lives, you know little of what these people are, really. They are strangers to you. The French were less strangers to me than they once were.

"It was a blunder to kill the Rosenbergs," Marie said.

"Maybe. It seemed to me to be too late for anything else to be done," I said.

The waiter brought our orders. I was having coffee and Marie was having tomato juice.

We sat back. Gradually, a state of dreamy relaxation took hold of me. Time, which I so often feel as an oppressive force that could rob me, now appeared to have stopped. It vanished from my mind, and it did not press on my nerves. I watched the people, now and then talked to Marie, and gazed at the tower across the street.

I noticed a grim young man coming along. He carried a bundle of papers under his arm, and I recognized him. He sold a paper called for the only real revolution, the revolution of youth against age. He often sold his paper, *Le Soulèvement des Jeuneusses* in front of the Deux Magots. Sometimes, I saw him selling also, on the Champs Elysées.

He stepped off the curb for about five feet, raised his

paper and began to shout about it and about the revolution of youth. He spoke slowly, and his voice was slightly deep and unpleasant. He was seedily dressed.

Three *flics* slowly closed in on him. It could have been like a scene in a movie. One of the blue-caped cops came directly behind him. The other two were on either flank. They came slowly, steadily and somewhat casually.

The young man began to proclaim that he was against the Communists. Five or six of the people sitting at the table called out to him, and Marie joined them in giving warning. But as if mesmerized by his own words, he went on talking. His head was rigid and his face expressed only fanaticism.

The cops grabbed him, and two of them quickly gave him the bum's rush across the street. His papers flew out of his hands. The third cop followed them. People on the sidewalk and at the café tables called out in protest. But the young man was in the van. It moved off.

"He did not do anything. And I hear him say he is not Communist," Marie said.

The people in the café talked more excitedly.

"They'll beat him up. The police always beat a man up when they arrest him," Marie said.

"There's the patron," I remarked. I was merely making conversation.

Marie looked indifferently at a smallish Frenchman in a black suit: he wore a white shirt, a black four-in-hand tie, and he had gray hair and a small gray moustache.

"He was the patron in the early thirties the first time I came here."

"Yes," Marie said rather indifferently.

The café was very noisy. Conversation was mounting. I watched people pass along the sidewalk and speculated about them. They seemed calm and un-worried. This did not mean much. A person can be torn with cares, problems and anxieties, and yet walk along the street as though he were the most unruffled person in the world. But nonetheless, I still felt that there was a calmness in these people, and I almost envied them. I did not feel calm myself, but I wanted to.

I tried to think of something to say to Marie but could think of nothing but the Rosenberg case. Marie and I had talked of it, and I had said all that I had to say of the case. There was resentment in me because of French reactions. I looked at Marie. She was French. I warned myself that I must not allow my resentment of the French reaction to the Rosenberg case to color my feelings toward her.

But I sat there, loving the night and feeling somewhat alien. Here I was in Paris, and I recalled how once I had loved the city. It was not the Rosenberg case and French hysteria alone which had affected me. In fact, I did not know that had affected me and was leading to changes in feeling and attitude. I thought of America far away, and a spell of loneliness came over me. I looked out at the big square, the old tower, and the bright big sky.

"It was stupid to kill the Rosenbergs," Marie said.

"Maybe. They helped bring it on themselves."

"In France, we had the Dreyfus case. Many Frenchmen think of the Rosenbergs like Dreyfus."

I knew that. But, I didn't want to talk more about the Rosenbergs. I closed up and was nontalkative. Glancing about, I saw many people talking, and there were many interested faces.

"If Eisenhower made a gesture," Marie began.

"I don't see how he could bend to pressure from other countries," I answered.

"It makes the French feel little, like worms. It makes the French feel that they don't count."

This was getting us onto thin ice. In Europe, I couldn't quite fully be a human being. I was an American.

"It's not just the Communists—many French, not Communist, did not want to see them killed in an electric chair."

"I know it."

"It was a blunder. It helps the Communists."

Some friends joined us. One was the brother of the aspirant to *chef de cabinet* whom we had seen walking by some minutes before. Another was a steel-faced, prematurely gray man who was making a fortune by running a private school in North Africa, and who, also, had been working on a book on Proust for about twenty-five years. And there was Danielle, the wife of a man in the export business. She was about forty and neither attractive nor unattractive in appearance, but she was a friendly and pleasant woman. She and her husband had lived in America for about six years, and she sometimes said that she was raising her daughter, a girl of eleven, in the American way. She meant that she was more permissive than the majority of French parents would be.

Danielle spoke of the Rosenberg case. She could not understand why the Americans had executed Julius and Ethel Rosenberg. Marie repeated that it had been a political blunder.

"It was so long," Danielle said.

I didn't quite understand what she meant, and asked her what had been so long. She answered that it had been so long that they had been in jail.

"It was cruel."

"Yes, that was cruel," Marie said.

"That was because of the number of appeals," I explained.

"In France, that would never be," Danielle said.

"Whether they were guilty or innocent, the delay was only because of the processes and safeguards of the American courts," I explained.

"But weren't they innocent?" Danielle asked with a look of surprise and wonder on her face.

"No, I don't think so," I answered.

Danielle continued to stare at me in surprise. The others talked in French about Proust and did not pay any heed to our conversation.

"But Dreyfus."

"The Dreyfus case has no relationship to this one."

"Dreyfus was innocent."

"I think so."

"And Sacco and Vanzetti?" Danielle asked.

"I think they were innocent."

"And you don't think the Rosenbergs were innocent?"

"No, I don't."

"Why?"

"I read the full reports of the case in the newspapers, and I am convinced of their guilt."

"They were Communists," Marie said.

Danielle looked at her in surprise.

"I know Communists," she said. "But I am not Communist. Did the Americans kill them because they were Communist?"

I sighed. I had been over all of this a number of times in the days prior to the execution, and on every occasion I would feel only frustration. Needless to say, I had had nothing to do with the case, and was in no way involved or responsible. But because of the simple fact that I was an American, Europeans talked to me as if I were responsible, and if I told them what I honestly thought— which invariably I tried to do—they would tell me or indicate to me that they understood how I felt it necessary to defend America. And so it would happen again. I wished we might talk of something else.

I wished this especially because Danielle was not truly interested in politics and did not have any opinions of her own on political questions. She had returned to France from America with vague dissatisfactions. She thought that Americans were materialistic and uncultured.

But Danielle kept asking me questions about the Rosenbergs, and I tried patiently to answer them. I explained that I should have liked to have seen them reprieved in the same sense that I should like to see anyone doomed to execution reprieved. But I was convinced that they were guilty of the charges made against them, and they had had a fair trial. Also I was convinced that they had been Communist spies. But my explanations meant nothing. She would come back to assertions of their innocence and to remark about being for the Negro and the worker, and against McCarthyism. This went on for a long time. Then she and her other friends left.

Marie and I sat for a few more minutes and we also left. By the curb near the café, I saw the car of the man with the moustache. The police still had him. He had wasted the evening for himself and the three people who were with him. I stopped, looked at the car and burst out laughing. Then we got into the Citroën and drove to the Right

Bank; Marie let me out on the Champs Elysées near my hotel. It was still lit up and crowded. I stood looking at the people go by, and then I walked to my hotel. I went to bed and lay thinking, France and America, Dreyfus, Sacco and Vanzetti, the abbey of Saint Germain des Prés, past and present and future. It was June. A June night had passed. A tranquil day and evening had come and gone in the history of man. But what was underneath that tranquility and what awaited us in the future. I fell asleep pondering, wondering and thinking, but arriving at no conclusions.

It's Cold in the Alps

The boat is pitching and rolling something fierce, and I don't know why I ain't seasick. Eloise always upbraided me about my speech, but, then, Eloise always upbraided me. I guess that's why I married her. I don't know if that's so or not, but it sounds okay. And it seems kind of funny to me. I like to say funny things, but Eloise never thought anything I said was funny. Maybe that's why I married her, too.

To tell the truth, I don't know why I married her. And now she's left me all in the dark, and I'm going home alone on the same boat that we came over on on our honeymoon. And I don't know how I feel about it either. I guess I don't know nothing from nothing.

I remember saying that, coming over on this same boat, and Eloise said to me: "Dear, don't use a double negative."

"Dear," I said, "it's triple."

"What in the name of creation are you talking about?" she asked me in one of her haughty manners. Eloise had many manners, and they were all haughty.

"Negatives—triple negatives," I answered.

"I thought you were talking about baseball," she said.

What I want to do here is to tell my story, but I don't know where to begin.

I met Eloise in college, and one thing led to another, and we got engaged. That was two years ago. We got married, and the big idea we had for our honeymoon was to take an automobile trip to Italy and to go over the Alps. All the way across the ocean, that was one of the main things we talked about when we didn't talk the kind of turtle-dove talk I guess all newlyweds talk. In England, we still talked about this. Then we went to France. We

liked Paris. It's a beautiful city, but it was in Paris that
things began to go sour. Anyway, that's the way I see it
most of the time. Sometimes I think that things were
always sour between us, even with the turtle-dove talk and
the billing-and-cooing and the rest of it.

You see, I did like it in Paris. Only Eloise wouldn't let
me like it. Over and over again she told me I didn't appreciate Paris, and, well, I did. We went to the Louvre. Now
that's something to see, especially the Venus de Milo. You
know, I'd take that Venus de Milo even without her arms,
only I didn't tell that to Eloise, of course. Well, Eloise
didn't like the way I pronounced the name, the Louvre.
She said I pronounced it like it was "Louver," not
"Louvre."

"Listen, honey, I ain't a Frenchman," I told her after
she reminded me for the sixth or seventh time that I was
mispronouncing the name.

Just on this one question of pronunciation alone, she
almost gave me an inferiority complex. I don't know if I
am right or wrong about this whole matter, but it seems
to me I'm right when I say that Eloise didn't want me to
appreciate nothing and wanted me to be a loogin. Eloise
used to burn my tail on my double negatives, and this
was my fault because I really knew better.

I remember our wedding. It hasn't much to do with
double negatives, except that there's no mistaking the fact
that it certainly turned out to be a double negative. My
old man is a big insurance broker, and he's well-heeled.
And I got an income from my grandmother. That's how I
am traveling first class and why Eloise and I stayed in
first-class hotels.

Eloise looked pretty and innocent in her white wedding
dress, with her veil and the flowers in her arms, and everybody said what a fine-looking couple we were, and they
spoke of how our honeymoon would be like a dream. Well,
I thought so too. Or at least, I think I thought so. I didn't
think much. I guess no man thinks much at his own wedding. Maybe if he did, he'd think too much.

Walking down the aisle of the church with the music
playing and our friends looking at us, the two of us the
center of attention and something to be envied, and some

of my buddies thinking of what I'd copped off—because Eloise looked pretty enough to be worth copping off—I was thrilled. But my head was in a fog, and I wanted the ceremonies over and done with. I was afraid I'd do the wrong thing, and even then I knew Eloise well enough to know that if I made a blunder there would be sixty-six kinds of hell to pay. This was a bigger moment for her than it was for me. I did everything all right, but I did it like a sleepwalker. The ceremony was really impressive, and I don't want to give the impression that it meant nothing to me. It did. In fact, it was beautiful. But it seemed to me beautiful in a way that music seems to me beautiful. I fall into a daze and I am far away and the music is far away, but I and the music are not far away in the same place—if you know what I mean. I am out of this world at one end, and the music is out of this world at the other. I hear it across the world. It's something like that kind of feeling, anyway, and I felt more or less like that at my own wedding.

But I won't go into the past, because I want to get to the Alps. I don't know if I'm glad or not glad that I ever got there. I can't be because I don't know if I'm glad or not about what happened between Eloise and me. And it was the Alps. That's where it happened.

Beautiful as Paris was, we wanted to get to the Alps. I say "we," but I don't know for sure if it was we, or only I. I wanted to. Why? Something fixed the Alps in my mind. As I say, everything wasn't hotsy-totsy and turtle-dove on our so-called honeymoon. I don't know what it was that made me think of the Alps as the land of heart's desire and everything else. I don't particularly like or dislike mountains. Somehow I got this bug. Everything before we got to the Alps was preliminary. The Alps were going to change our lives. Everything I had ever wanted to happen would happen when we got there. I was dense, as you'll soon see as quick as I can take you back to the Alps with me. I was thick.

I bought a Citroën for something like sixteen hundred dollars. It was a bit of a headache because I guess you can't do business as simple in Europe as you can in America. I was told by an American I met at the American Express Company on the Rue Scribe that you have got to grease the palms of the Frogs if you want to get any business done, so I greased this dealer's palm to the tune of a hundred dollars. And there was the headache of getting everything filled out. In Europe your car has to have a passport—that is, you've got to have a car passport. Well, I got that all attended to with much confusion and time-wasting.

And did I have my headaches driving in that Paris traffic! I not only had the French to contend with. I also had my sweet little Eloise. I don't know which gave me the bigger headache, the French or Eloise. That would be a hard one to answer. The traffic in Paris is like anarchy. I never knew what anarchism was except that I'm against it and it's radical, but I never knew what an anarchist was. Now I know. An anarchist is a Frenchman driving an automobile in gay Paree. Don't get me wrong and think I mean the French are bad drivers. They couldn't be. If they were, they'd all have been dead long ago. I tell you, and I mean it, it's something to drive in Paris traffic for the first few times before you get used to it. It's something to look at.

Just before I got my car, I was standing on the sidewalk at the Place de l'Opéra which is one of the busiest places in Paris. There was an American G.I. standing beside me, just gaping wide-eyed at the passing traffic with a cigarette hanging loosely from one corner of his mouth. And, not changing that look of complete surprise and fascination on his face, he says dead pan: "All I want to see is one of them Frenchmen let loose in a car in Times Square at the rush hour."

And, brother, I thought, them's my sentiments too.

The French drive individually, and let the devil take the hindmost. But I'd almost say there is no hindmost. So every driver watches out for himself, and they speed and shoot along, and you see the damndest traffic mixups, while the cars go shooting all over the streets. The *Places* in Paris are mostly round, and the cars shoot around them like a crazy wheel or a crazy merry-go-round, speeding if they can, every driver seeming to want to cut in ahead of every other driver, and no driver letting any other get ahead of him if he can possibly help it. And mixed up in all of this shooting and scooting traffic of cars, with the horns tooting and blaring away, are the bicycle drivers. Say, if you think a Frenchman on a bicycle will get out of the way of a car, brother, you aren't just mistaken, you're plenty mistaken, and I mean *plenty*. Because the bicycle riders think they've got the right of way. And, too, in the traffic, just as likely as not, you'll see, right in the center of it all—of all the cars, not to mention the bicycles, not to speak of the motorbikes and motorcycles—there will be an old cripple in a wheelchair going peacefully along his way as if there weren't a car within a hundred meters of him, working away with his hands, just taking a peaceful ride in his bicycle-like wheelchair or whatever you call it, not minding the cars in the least and just letting them get out of his way and stay out of it.

Now, not only did I have to get myself conditioned or oriented to drive in this kind of traffic, but I also had to do it with Eloise at my side. She rode me plenty on the whole trip, but when I was driving, especially in Paris, she just rode herd on me. She was never done with telling me to watch myself and what I was doing, and when I would say that was precisely and exactly what was on my mind, why then she would tell me to watch what the other fellow was doing. And she kept saying to me that she'd thought I was a better driver than I was proving myself to be. And then, too, there were directions and getting lost. She'd look at the maps. In Paris, you can buy a damned good book of the streets with maps of every *arrondisement,* and she'd look at these whenever we had to find out where we were going and how to get there. Invariably she'd get things wrong, and just as invariably she'd blame me and say that it was my fault.

But all of these difficulties notwithstanding, I learned to drive and to get about, and we got everything arranged so we could get out of Paris and on to the Alps. And just like Dale Carnegie or somebody else said that life begins at forty, so I thought that life and love would begin in the Alps. I guess I was sentimental and romantic. But there's the way I felt. Maybe I talked to Eloise too much about

the Alps. But at times, anyway, she acted like she was
looking forward to getting to the Alps herself.

Now the *Queen Mary* is plowing through the Atlantic
Ocean, and all this seems strange to me and far away, and
there are moments when it seems as if it never happened
and as if I had read it all in a story. I don't know quite
how to explain my feelings here, and I don't like to say I
am sad and disappointed. So how will I put it? I look at
the ocean as the boat goes on and on, and I can only see
the water and the sky, nothing else, no land. Every minute
the ocean is different, with the waves on it. It's moving all
the time. The waves are rolling and rolling, and the swell
about the boat is churning and the water is foaming. And
away from the swell it's gray and the waves roll over the
ocean, and it makes me lonely. And the sky seems so big.
I never saw the sky as big as it looks over the ocean. The
sky makes me lonely. I wonder, now, if Eloise was with
me, would I feel as lonely looking at the ocean and the
sky as I do now; and if not Eloise, if someone else was
with me, would I feel this way? And that brings me back
to our trip to the Alps.

I expected I was going to see something and see it not
alone. I was going to see something beautiful with Eloise,
and that when the two of us saw something beautiful together, why, it would make our lives beautiful. This is
what romance means or, anyway, it's what romance has
always meant to me. Of course, I never talked much about
romance and I always laughed at it cynically. But inside
of myself, I wasn't cynical. I always wanted this romance
in my life, and I lived for the day when it would happen.
It would change my life and make it . . . well, yes, make it
beautiful. I might as well admit it, since it's the truth.
When I became engaged to Eloise, I thought that I had
found what I had lived all of my life for. But then, there
we were on our honeymoon, and I was still waiting for
something wonderful to happen.

Sometimes I had the feeling I had done something to
Eloise. I'm sure you know what I am talking about here,
and once, when we were driving in Paris over somewhere
on the Right Bank near the Bois de Boulogne, I had the
thought that she wanted me to feel that way. I became

afraid that Eloise and I had something to be ashamed of in common, a secret between us that made us ashamed. And that made me, maybe, more ashamed than she was.

"Watch what you're doing," she shouted at me just as I was having these thoughts.

I put my foot on the brake and stopped the car pronto, and it's damned good I did, or there would have been a collision. A Frenchman in another car yelled at me in French.

"No parlor the English," I yelled at him.

"You don't have to be a vulgar clown. You could have killed me," Eloise shouted at me, sore as a cat.

She stayed sore at me for an hour. It's no fun on your honeymoon when your wife is always yelling and getting sore at you, and then that sometimes gets you boiled up in turn yourself. Eloise got sore more times than is compatible with a joyous honeymoon.

Well, anyway, that's the way it was, and I kept looking forward to my honeymoon when I was already on it. I guess that didn't help much, though of course I didn't say this in so many words to Eloise. But I didn't enjoy myself from day to day as I guess I should have, or at least have tried to do. Of course, Eloise, with her disposition, wasn't a big help in that department. I never knew what to do to please her. Sometimes that would get me to thinking of what I should do to satisfy her or at least not to rile her up. But I never knew for sure how to behave and what to say to her.

But my fervor to get to the Alps did catch on with her a bit because she too talked sometimes about our trip and about how she wanted to get on with it. And it was her idea of sleeping out, and she began to talk about how we would do this in the Alps. It seemed all right to me, although I did say once or twice that it might be a little cold sleeping that way, but I only half meant this. I really said it because I didn't cotton to the idea, but I didn't want to tell her that in so many words for fear that it would get her even more riled up. And maybe I was right, because when I did half-heartedly tell her that it might be cold in the Alps, why she just hooted me down.

Our car was fixed up so you could pull the seats back

and sleep in it, and I went to a department store and we bought blankets and equipment to sleep out in. Well, I had some kind of vague uneasiness about this, but I said nothing more and forgot it. I got maps and guidebooks of France and I studied the maps and I wanted to get off. I was enthusiastic.

The morning we left, I wanted to get an early start, and Eloise agreed with me. It was all planned. I was up at seven. We'd packed the night before—that is, I packed and Eloise did some of her packing. I tried to get her to do more of it, but I failed. That morning Eloise was sleepy and said she'd get up when breakfast came. So I got up and started humming a tune while I was shaving. I felt that good. Our quarrels and the times that Eloise got riled and all of the riding herd she'd done on me—well, that was all bygones. So I hummed while I shaved. But you can guess what happened. Eloise didn't like that. It woke her up.

"But, darling, you have to get up anyway."

"Don't be an uncivilized American. You're in France," she told me.

We were going to be together all day in the car, and I didn't want her starting out in an ugly mood, so I stopped humming. Breakfast was brought up, and we ate. I wanted to talk about the trip. I remember saying: "I'd like to make at least three hundred kilometers today."

"Don't worry. I'll be up and I won't delay you," she shot at me.

It was as if she had read my mind. I tried to tell her that I wasn't worried about her being ready, when that was just what I was thinking. That was one thing about Eloise and I in our brief so-called marriage and our so-called honeymoon. She always had the jump on me whenever she wanted it. Now, I think maybe it was because she's much smarter than I am, and then, maybe it's because she wanted it that way, whereas I wanted to get along with her . . . I don't know.

But to continue my story. Eloise didn't get right out of bed after breakfast. I got nervous and didn't know what to do with myself. I kept sitting down on the bed or on a chair, getting up, sitting down, getting up, walking about the room which wasn't very big, looking at my wrist watch, and getting more and more nervous.

Eloise noticed me and said, a bit cuttingly too, if I remember correctly: "Dear, don't be so jittery. The Alps will still be there."

"I know they will," I answered, not thinking of what I was saying, and then right off I felt like a damned fool. I must have had some kind of funny look on my face because I remember Eloise saying: "You look stupid."

I got sore, but instead of giving her an argument I went into the bathroom. So Eloise immediately knocks on the door and tells me that if I'm so anxious to get started, why do I hog the bathroom.

Anyway, I had to wait over two hours for her to get ready. We left our hotel at 11:15. And I got misdirected and went to the wrong *Porte*. That wasted more time. We weren't outside the limits of Paris until 12:30. Of course, this didn't matter too much, because what Eloise said was true—the Alps would always be there and it didn't matter if we reached them on one day or the next. It was just my anxiousness to be started and, also, I felt that it wasn't fair of Eloise to stall me the way she did for no good reason. I was sore. I didn't have much to say for some time. But Eloise didn't seem to mind. She sat beside me just as calm as though she had done nothing at all to rile me up.

"Aren't you satisfied?" she asked me as we were going across a stone bridge spanning the Marne.

"I didn't say anything."

"You're certainly sociable on your honeymoon."

"I was just driving and watching where I was going."

"You got lost once already."

"Anybody can get lost in Paris. Didn't the cop give me a wrong steer about the Porte Vincennes?"

"You would have gotten lost without the police to help you misdirect yourself, dear. It's just that you don't have any sense of direction, darling." Eloise just didn't give me credit for anything.

Well, anyway, we got on. I hit up a good speed, and I liked the car. A Citroën is a damned good car for my money. It holds the road nicely and it took us over the Alps and into Italy and, I tell you, it's a damned good car. It doesn't have all the power of an American car, of course, and I wouldn't take it to an American car, but for my money it's a nice job. And I enjoyed shooting along at eighty, ninety, a hundred kilometers an hour.

And France is beautiful. The whole country must be just like a garden. It affected me, and it affected Eloise, too. The country is so rich, and the soil is just rich, that's all, rich. And driving by, I thought of how this land had been cultivated for centuries and how the peasants who cultivate it had learned to get just about everything they can out of that earth. It was warm and sunny and just mighty beautiful, shooting along with few cars on the road and seeing this rich land in cultivation all around us. It was warm and brown and almost golden and green, and the brown plowed earth was brown in the sunshine, and the fields of crops—of wheat and of vegetables—waving a little in the wind.

Then there were hills and trees. We would drive along a road with trees lining it, sometimes with the trees standing, tall and straight one by the other, and the leaves would cover the road so that we would drive in shade. It was wonderful, and it affected Eloise, because a number of times she said to me: "It's simply divine."

Now and then we would sing. I was happy. It was as if our honeymoon had really begun, and the little squabblings and Eloise's dissatisfactions with me back there in Paris all seemed unimportant. I forgot all about them. I just drove on, and odd thoughts would pop in and out of my head. I thought, driving along a straight road lined with trees, how here we were, two Americans, not long married and honeymooning in France. It was too surprising and too good to be true.

We stopped in some little town for coffee—that is, *café* —at about three or three-thirty. I liked that. But there was a sour note here.

"Let's send postcards," I said.

"Don't you think our friends are tired of receiving postcards from us?"

"Why should they be?"

"If you don't know, why should I tell you?" Eloise snapped at me, talking to me as if I was the biggest dumb-sock in the world.

We sat outside a little café in this little French village having coffee. I don't remember the name of the village. I wanted to remember as many names as I could, but they've all gotten mixed up in my mind and I can't remember hardly any of them. Many of these French villages are alike, anyway, and when you get in the French countryside you find that the villages are nearly all dirty and the peasants look like they were living in some past century, not the twentieth century. It's different from Switzerland. There the villages and everything else are clean as a whistle. But in a French village there are people and cows and chickens all on the main street, and sometimes you can't get away from the smell of manure. I said this, sitting in a café with Eloise.

It was about three-thirty, and it was a hot day. I was tired and I wanted to sit back and relax and enjoy our rest. But she angrily shot something or other at me about my being one of these American tourists who wanted to find everything American wherever I went. I didn't answer her because I didn't want any argument. To myself I said quietly:—Eloise, darling, this is our honeymoon. She kept needling me about being a tourist.

"Darling, aren't we both tourists?" I asked her. So she got really sore. She only interrupted her argument with me because she had to go to the W.C.

I sat there, alone and depressed. Eloise had gotten riled up again over nothing at all. I think that I'm really a good-natured guy and all of my friends think the same, and in college I was pretty popular because I had the reputation for being witty and easygoing. But I get sore, too, and I was getting sore. I just felt that Eloise had been unfair to me. Hell, if there is or isn't manure on the street of a French village that we were spending a half hour in on our way to somewhere else, and if you do or you don't smell that manure, is it any reason, either way, for two honeymooners to have a dog fight? Sometimes when Eloise would make a crack at me, this would just wash off like water off a duck's back. I wouldn't take it seriously.

But now and then it would get under my skin and get me sore. It would hurt my vanity, I guess. That's the way I felt in that café.

Two kids were watching me, a boy and a girl of about eight. They were barefooted and dirty, and they stared at me as if I was something very strange and not human. I wanted to talk to them, but I didn't know French, except I'd picked up a kind of taxicab-and-waiters' French so that I could order and get directions.

I said to the two kids: *"Comment allez-vous?"* I might just as well have been talking Greek to them. The boy was curly-haired and blond and blue-eyed. He flung a stream of French at me.

"What did you say?" I asked him. The two kids laughed. I pulled out a hundred-franc note and, holding it up, I said: "Here. *Ici. Voila.*"

The kids came forward and the boy snatched the money and, thanking me with an unbelieving expression on their faces, they ran off. They were cute kids. I like kids.

Then I became bitter because on the wall of a barn across from the little café, I read: "U.S. GO HOME."

Suddenly I wanted to go home. I didn't want to go to the Alps. I wanted to turn the car around, shoot back to Paris, and get the first boat for New York. I felt that I didn't belong in France, and that I was kidding myself about this whole trip, about my honeymoon and my marriage. I knew that I wasn't having a good time. I was far away from home, and I wished I was back, and I thought that maybe this was the way many Americans sometimes feel when they are in Europe. Anyway, if other American tourists did or didn't ever feel this way in Europe, I did. I just felt sunk, sunk.

Eloise came back from the W.C. She was angry about the toilet, and with reason. In many of the French toilets there are no seats and you stand up, and a number of them, especially when you get into the countryside, they smell like all hell. They just aren't sanitary. Yes, Eloise had a real gripe there, and I should have had enough sense to let her complain to her heart's content about French toilets, because then maybe she'd have gotten it all out of her system, at least for a while, and she wouldn't gripe at me. In fact, I did recognize this, but just the same I didn't have enough sense to keep my trap shut.

I said: "What the hell do you expect? You're not in America. Look at the charm you can see, instead of getting worked up because you don't find American plumbing over here."

Well, that was a dumb thing for me to have said. Eloise turned her hottest fire on me instead of on the French toilets. So I thought that we'd better be getting on. I paid the bill and we set off again.

I was still depressed. In a little while, with both of us silent, I got over the dumps. The pleasure of driving, of zooming the car along at a hundred kilometers an hour, and the beautiful countryside, all helped to get me out of my funk. And Eloise got less sore because now and then she would see something charming or attractive and comment on it.

Well, I can't give you a blow-by-blow and a kilometer-by-kilometer account of the trip, because if I do I'll never get to the Alps. But I do want to remark on how I liked it, driving on into the dying day, with the sun going down ahead of us and the color of the air and the sky and of everything changing, the two of us all alone together in the car, all alone in the world and in France; and the sky getting darker and the clouds becoming a soft pink and red; and the sun a deep orange and then a kind of glowing, burning red; and trees with the leaves greener and darker because the sun was going down; and a feeling I had that out there, beyond the sound of our car, it was quiet, silent, all was silent; and all of the color and this changing color was important, mighty important. I got a thrill out of it. And I got a thrill out of going on for a while when it had grown dark. I felt again how we were alone in the world. And I liked it, switching my lights all the time to signal ahead, and signaling with my switched lights to drivers coming toward me, and they doing the same thing. It was a language we were talking to one another with lights.

Finally we stopped in a town. I forget the name of the town except that it was pretty big—big, that is, for a French provincial town—and it is very old, and I think that its name begins with a "B," but I'm not certain of that. We shacked up at a hotel. It was all right, but it wasn't anything more than that. I was fagged out, and all I wanted was to take a bath and get some sleep. I was so tired that even if Eloise had been in one of her worst moods I wouldn't have been fazed because I wouldn't have even heard her for long. Five minutes after I was out of the bathtub and in bed, I was asleep.

We didn't get too late a start the next morning. We were on our way by nine. I might say that when I went down for breakfast there was a radio on, and I didn't believe I was really hearing what I heard. It couldn't be true, I thought, yet it was. Because on the radio I heard "Go U. Northwestern"—or is it "Go You Northwestern"? The café connected with the hotel was a sporting café, and I guess that was why I should have heard an American college song in that French provincial town. But it sure made me feel good.

Well, on that second day we made good progress, and it wasn't too long before we were climbing and in the French Alps. I got quite a kick out of this. I had reached the Alps. The climb wasn't so hard or difficult, and it wasn't at all like what we had in store for us. But the air was pure and clear, and there was a fine chill in it like the chill of autumn, with the wind blowing strong. The little mountain towns were different from the villages we'd passed through the day before, and the trees were tall and straight, and you passed places where trees had been cut, and you saw big newly cut logs by the side of the road. I was excited and disappointed. I wanted to stop and not go on, and I wanted to get on to the Swiss border. And the little towns or villages, some of them were dirty, and some of them were like resort or vacation towns. And the houses, they were different from the stone houses I'd been seeing. It was all so new. Of course, the countryside of France was new and different, too, but I had gotten used to it after driving for an hour or so. and I hadn't thought so much of it being new and different. And I never saw trees so straight and tall as I saw them and as I kept seeing them. It was as if everything I saw had a meaning and was important. And I had feelings that it isn't easy for me to express or describe. Maybe that's why I often wise-crack, because when you wisecrack and make jokes of things, you don't have to say what you feel about them. Don't get me wrong here. I don't think you should be a sourpuss and not have a sense of humor or anything like that. I only mean that sometimes you don't want to do this, but want to———well, you want to feel just what you do feel, if you get what I mean. I know I'm not making it too clear, but I am trying to give you some idea of what I am getting at and of the way I felt.

As the morning was passing and I was driving through the French Alps, I felt that I was in a world that had not been seen and discovered before by an American. I saw it as we went on, sometimes going fast, sometimes going slow, sometimes dragging along at a crawl behind a big truck or a big blue bus full of people. And I knew that I was only at the beginning of the Alps, and that I was going to see more and more, and that I was going to go higher.

Now, I told myself, it had begun. What I meant by it and by telling this to myself as I sat at the wheel of the Citroën going along at fifty kilometers taking a very sharp curve as I slowed down, was that life had become a dif-ferent thing and was going to go on being different—and better. My honeymoon was really started. Whatever it was that I was living to experience, now I was going to know it.

Eloise was mostly silent. Now and then she would say something about what we were seeing, about a scene where we could see off ahead or down one side of the road, a panorama of trees and fields sloping away from us with sun on it, shining, with patches of ground that was cultivated and little houses tucked in here and there and villages set in a spot with fields around them. Or she would tell me to watch my driving. But in the main we didn't say very much.

I wanted to say something. I wanted for us both to say something to each other that would make us feel closer together than we had ever felt before, closer than any two honeymooners had ever felt in the whole world. Yes, I wanted to say something that would make us feel not only that close, but would also give us the idea that we were a part of all of this we were seeing and that it all was part of this closeness we were feeling. I wanted us to feel like we were——well, in a way, one with the whole world. I wanted to think that the sun shining, and the sun getting lost behind a cloud, and the mist, and the sunny haze, and the tall straight trees standing on the sharp sides of the mountains that were falling away from the road, and the far, big stretches of mountains and slopes and fields and houses and patches of ground, and the mountains rising on the side, going up higher than we were, with their big straight tall green trees and the little terraces of marked-off cultivated ground—that all this was part of the way we felt ourselves to be one and together. I wanted to say something like this, but I couldn't, because I didn't know how to say it. And, well, yes—I was afraid to say it for fear that Eloise might laugh at me or make a snotty remark or just think that I was a sentimental dope.

Well, we went on. We were near Mont Jura, and I kept seeing the name Jura in the towns and villages. We were also getting close to the frontier, and this made me feel kind of nervous, because we would have to pass through customs. I don't know why I should have been nervous, because I wasn't smuggling anything. I wasn't taking anything for which I could be fined or anything like that. As I kept getting nearer the border, I started getting more worried. I couldn't stop myself from being this way, even though I knew that there was no reason why I should have any trouble. I couldn't understand myself. I kept speeding and not seeing the mountains, because I wanted to get over with the business of going through customs. My driving even got a bit reckless. I spun around a curve too fast.

Then I asked Eloise three times if she had her passport. She had plenty to say in answer to that question. I won't try to repeat it all here—in fact, I don't even remember it all. She really burned my ears. But I couldn't help myself. I still don't get it, why I should have been so nervous and worried about something like that, but I was.

I remember we stopped at a café in a village and had coffee and cheese, and the cheese was mighty good. They make it in the region. But I was still in that same state, and Eloise had more of her appropriate comments to make.

"You must take moving pictures serious," she told me.

Now that, I must say, was an odd remark. But by that time I had already gotten to understand Eloise well enough to know when something was coming, and I wasn't wrong.

"But why should you have such ideas as that about me?" I asked, but I was on the defensive because of my aforesaid nervous state about the customs.

"Why? You act just as though you might be some big international smuggler or black marketeer, the way you're carrying on about passing the French and Swiss customs. When you have nothing to hide or to smuggle!"

That she said with a cutting edge. Back in America they talk in the television commercials and on the radio about Gillette blades having the sharpest edges ever honed. Well, her tongue had a sharp edge and she sure honed it.

I was still on the defensive, but it was *touché* for her. Now, when I think about my so-called honeymoon and look back on it, it was *touché* for Eloise too damned many times.

I won't go on about this except to remark that it was nothing in particular to get through customs, although they did make me show my car passport, and they checked up on it carefully, because at the European borders they are watchful to see if anyone is trying to get over with a stolen car. They didn't even stamp our passports. I might say here that we had separate passports because Eloise wanted it that way, although most married Americans going to Europe would have one passport. But in Eloise's case that would have been an insult to her independence. She had to have a separate passport.

Well, that's how we got to Switzerland, anyway.

Switzerland was a change from France. We began to see some signs in German. And, of course, just everything in Switzerland was cleaner than it is in France. Switzerland is the cleanest country I've been in in my short life and with my limited travels. I was excited to be there. The scenery was so pretty; in fact, it was beautiful.

I drove on fast to Geneva. We did stop once and get out of the car to look down at a sweeping panorama and it snatched the breath right out of me. I just thought of how much beauty there was in the world. I put my arm around Eloise. There were other people there, a whole busload of them looking out at the panorama.

"There are people watching us," Eloise said, and that put something of a damper on me.

It was more exciting to get to Geneva than to go to some American city like Chicago or Cleveland, just as it was much more exciting to go to the Alps than it would be to see the Rocky Mountains. This is just because it's foreign and the people speak another language, I guess, and also because you've heard so much about these places in Europe, and you think that these are the places where history was made or historic events happened, more than you think the same thing about any places in America. The streets of Geneva were crowded. There were a lot of people on bicycles. I saw quite a few automobiles, so I could easily guess that the Swiss were prosperous. Many of the cars were American, too. And the Swiss were all pretty well dressed. The people seemed much better dressed than the French as a whole are. I wanted to buy a Swiss watch. Eloise told me I was a sucker, and I almost didn't buy the watch because of her and the way she ragged me. But I went ahead in spite of her and picked up a good watch for about a hundred francs, Swiss. That's a heck of a lot more than one hundred francs, French. As I bought it, I was mighty glad that the clerk in the little store didn't understand English and didn't therefore know what Eloise was saying to me. To say the least about it, it just wasn't complimentary.

We spent one day in Geneva, but I didn't enjoy it. Eloise didn't like the Swiss. Well, that was all right with me. I wouldn't say I either like or didn't like them. I don't know much about them. But she just acted like a wet blanket instead of like a bride. She didn't like the League of Nations Building or anything else, and when I showed any interest, her dislike was doubled.

I was glad when we drove out of Geneva on a sunny morning. I don't know what happened to Eloise, but she was ready at 7:30 A.M. And this was the day, too, the big day of our trip and of our honeymoon, because I had calculated that by night we would make the Alps and maybe reach the top of them.

We drove along the lake, out of Geneva toward Lausanne. The lake was quiet and the water was blue; and in some places, with the haze and the sun, the water so calm, and the trees and the little islands, why it was completely out of this world.

As we hit it along at about eighty kilometers, Eloise said that she wanted to sleep out in the Alps. I didn't say anything. It was all right with me.

Well, we got to some town, I forget the name of it, and I found out that we were only forty-eight kilometers from the Colle De Simplon where we were going across the Alps. I was keen. We went on and I kept getting keener every minute, and at the same time I was almost feeling a disappointment that I would hardly admit to myself. There I was, driving on, every minute getting closer to what I had been looking forward to seeing, but this wasn't bringing about any change between Eloise and me.

As for the Alps—well, anything anybody tells you about them is true. As we started to climb, you could see so many magnificent and tremendous views, mountains rising ahead of you on either side, with the tall green trees straight on the sides of the mountains. In some places it was like a wall of trees. And the views looking down— seeing the slopes and plains and trees, seeing little houses half hidden away, and the patches of earth, and the roads here and there below, and the richness of color, and the sweep of the declining landscape—it kept taking my breath away.

Then driving was a terrific thrill. It was a bit dangerous because of the curves, when you couldn't see ahead and didn't know if another car or bus was coming around the same curve from the other direction. But you honked your horn, and other drivers did the same. There were buses, too, and they took up almost all of the road. I was worried for fear that one would be coming around a turn from the opposite direction, but I had good luck all the way. And there were the sharp declines when I took some curves on the outside of the road. Just a few feet to my right the mountain would go down straight. That gave you a thrill because, if you were going around a curve blind and a car or a bus were coming the other way and you didn't keep your wits and watch the road and keep the car in good control, then you could go down and that would mean the lights would go out for you. Also, the road wasn't too good. It was a tense as well as a thrilling experience. I couldn't look at and see as much as I wanted to of the scenery because I had to keep my eyes on that road.

But what I did see! I never saw anything like it in my life. We climbed slowly, as it was getting to the end of the day. I saw the sweep of the land below as the sun got red and went down, and the sharp slope and decline of the mountain, and the plateaus with the little houses way down below and far away, and peaks off in the distance standing like giants against the sky. And the green of the trees at twilight, and then the curves, the surprises, with your seeing one view that couldn't be more magnificent, and then coming on another that was, and you just felt awe—that's all, awe. And the mountain streams, the sound of the water, with sometimes a stream by the side of the road. The streams below, catching the sun before it went down and all shining and sparkling. And I liked the sound of the running water, a sound that was its own music. I tell you, I never saw anything like it. I'm not the religious type, but I felt religious. At times I thought the whole world was a church and I was worshiping in it. I felt all kinds of things that I can't know how to tell you about or describe, and I'm not even going to try.

And it was all the more thrilling and exciting because I was driving, and I never in my life felt the same way about driving as I did then. Would my car make the climb? Would my hand brake work if I needed to use it in the climb so that we wouldn't go rolling backward down the mountain? Would I be able to stay on the road? I knew that I would, but there was still that fear. So many of the declines were so sudden, so abrupt, so steep. And they were right there, a few feet away from the road where you had to take long acute curves on the outside. At times I would be afraid even to allow myself as much as one glance at the scenery for fear I'd tumble us down the mountainside. Then I'd make myself take that glance. I had tingles of fear all over. I felt my spine and my nerves quivering. And I was keen, too. I felt as if I were small and nothing at all, a weak little man here in the presence of these mountains that had stood silent and mighty for centuries before me and would stand mighty and silent for hundreds of years after me. But I also felt powerful, with my hands on the wheel controlling that Citroën, and climbing slowly, steadily, going on up, up, taking a curve and another curve.

And there was a silence in the mountains. I heard the wind and the sounds of the streams and at the same time, there was my feeling of silence. The sun was silent. Those peaks off to my right, to my left, and ahead of me, they were silent. Inside myself, I felt the richest silence in the world.

Eloise was scared. She was so frightened she often couldn't look down. She kept telling me to watch what I was doing and to keep my eyes on the road, which was just what I did. She was like one big knot that you couldn't untie. I never saw her that way before.

"I'll get you over the mountains, dear. Relax," I told her at one point when we had to make a pretty steep climb and go around another blind tunneled curve.

As I said, the sun was going down as we drove on up. It was beginning to get chilly. The scenes seemed to change. I had a feeling of sadness and greatness. The scenes, especially with the sun going down, made me feel lonely. The Alps, the peaks, the stone houses to be seen here and there, a car every now and then passing us—all this, too, gave me that lonely feeling. And I felt that I hadn't seen enough. I had missed something. I don't know what it was that I had missed, but it was something. The peaks around us, with the green of the trees now so much darker, seemed to me to be brooding and melancholy over all the troubles and sorrows and deaths of the centuries. Also, it was as though something sad were going on in the Alps. It was the ending of the day. The air growing gray and dark and a chill coming over all of these scenes. The sky was getting still darker and very blue. Then the sun was gone. There was pink in the sky, off away from us in clouds over a tall peak. We were still climbing slowly, and it was sad.

Eloise was quiet. I didn't say anything. I mostly kept my eyes glued on that road. Out of the corner of my eye, now and then, I caught glances of more than the road, more than what I saw ahead of me. I was tight and drawn, or maybe just alert. I was driving well and that was a pleasure, too. The car was going smoothly. It was holding the road. I blew the horn loud.

"I always jump when you do that," Eloise said.

"I've got to, darling," I answered.

We were slowly edging around another blind curve on the outside of the road with a terrific decline on the right. I edged over more toward the center, just to be doubly careful.

I honked loud again. Was there a car coming? We edged around slowly, and then had a straight stretch ahead.

"I know you have to," Eloise said.

"What's that you said, darling?" I asked her.

"You don't pay attention to what I say. You take me for granted already, just as if I'd been married to you for years."

"I don't. I was watching the road. This is hazardous driving." I remember that when I said this I wanted her to hand me an orchid for the way I was driving.

"I know you have to honk that horn but you don't pay any attention to me any more. There isn't any gallantry in your soul."

I couldn't answer her because there was another blind curve ahead and I had to take it on the outside, with the steep almost straight decline only about three or four feet away from the edge. Eloise made me almost jittery. I put my finger on the horn to blow it again. I hesitated. I didn't want to because of her. I honked loudly.

Well, that is the way it went. It got darker and chillier.

"We'll sleep out tonight," Eloise suddenly said.

"It's too chilly."

"Are you afraid?"

"It's not my being afraid—it's chilly and it won't be comfortable."

I was plenty tired. I'd done a lot of driving in three days, coming all of the way from Paris to almost the top of Colle de Simplon, which is something like twenty-four hundred kilometers high. I knew that when I stopped driving for the day I was going to be done in. I felt groggy and wanted a warm bath and a soft bed.

"After all you said about the Alps, now you're backing out on me."

"I'm not backing out on anything. Aren't we here? Didn't I get you here without any mishaps?"

"I knew it. There's no romance . . . oh, watch what you're doing!"

I was watching, and I drew over to the side of the road and stopped. A big blue bus was coming up the other way. I waited for it to pass. Some of the passengers waved and I waved back and yelled: *"Comment ça va?"* That's more French that I learned.

My back was aching, and I felt stiff. My eyes were beginning to feel heavy. I was hungry, and I felt dusty and dirty. The day's drive had been more of a grind than I had realized. Yes, I wanted to eat, bathe, and just hit the hay. I was too fagged to care about seeing any more. I had seen all of the scenery, all of the mountains, all of the peaks, all of the vistas, panoramic views, and sweeping landscapes I wanted to see for one day, not to speak of the clouds and the sky. The moon was out now, bright and full and white and silver, but I didn't care.

I crawled the car along, driving more carefully and cautiously just because I was tired.

"I'm hungry," I said.

"Do you think that you are the only person in the world who has a stomach?"

"My stomach is so empty that I'm not thinking of anybody else's stomach, darling."

"No, you wouldn't think of mine."

"I'm not telling you, am I, that you have to think of my stomach instead of your own, am I?"

"You're just vulgar and selfish."

I don't know what called for that and I didn't take it too seriously, but I had one of those passing thoughts that I ought to have taken seriously, and it was that Eloise didn't really love me or even have any use for me. But I didn't hang on to that thought, even though now, I think—in fact, I know—that I had something there.

I didn't say anything more for a few minutes. I crept the car on up. We went along a ledge, with breathtaking, wonderful views below and way down on our right. I saw a few lights in little houses. They seemed romantic to me and made me even more lonesome. I thought of how far away I was from home and my own country. I wanted this trip to be over with and for us to be back in New York and settled, with myself in the advertising business. I think I forgot to tell you that I'm going back to a promising job in the advertising business.

Eloise was not only silent—she was angrily silent. You would have thought that I had done something to her other than merely be myself. But last night on the ship here, I was watching the dancing. I couldn't find anyone to dance with me, and I sat feeling lonesome and out of it, and hearing songs that I liked, and that made me . . . well, moody and more lonesome. Then, suddenly, I had the idea that it was just me—me, myself and I—and my being just myself that Eloise didn't like and couldn't tolerate. And I thought of our drive and of just that part of our drive and that time of day that I am telling you about now, and of how I felt so lonesome at just those moments and of how I wanted to be back home in America. And I thought, too, how I would probably never have had all kinds of thoughts and feelings and moods if I hadn't gone to Europe.

Well, we took another curve and climbed again, and I wondered how soon we'd find a hotel. I said to my wife —maybe I ought to call her my so-called wife—but anyway, I said: "I wonder how soon we'll find a hotel?"

"You're afraid, aren't you?"

I was surprised. I confess I didn't immediately catch on to what she was talking about. I didn't know what to say. If a woman tells a man he's afraid—and especially his wife—on that man's honeymoon, well, naturally it hurts. Everybody is afraid sometimes, and certainly women are, and I'm no exception to the fears of the well-known human race. But as things go, I think that there are plenty who are more afraid than I am. Eloise's needling got under my skin. It hurt. It kept hurting particularly because I was moody, I guess.

"I'm not afraid," I said.

"You're walking out on me."

"How am I walking out on you?"

"You promised me you'd sleep out in the Alps."

This had gone clean out of my mind, but when she brought up the subject I knew that I didn't want to sleep in the car and be cold and uncomfortable, especially because I was done in from the day's drive, as I've already told you. But she put it in such a way that I couldn't say I didn't want to do it, but just wanted to find a hotel and get a decent night's sleep.

"Why are you talking about a hotel?"

"We've got to eat, don't we?"

She didn't answer. That was the way she was on our entire honeymoon. If I proved her wrong or gave her a good answer when she needled me, she just turned tight as a clam.

Well, we went on. It was getting darker and it was really chilly. Soon, when I had come to believe that we still had a long way to travel before I could find a place that would be serving grub, we came to a hotel. It was at a curve in the road and was built up on a little natural platform on the side of the mountain. I forget the name, but it was still Switzerland. There were buildings on either side of the road, a two-story hotel on one side and a two-story building with the restaurant on the other.

I stopped the car by a small and old garage, and as we got out Eloise said: "We can park the car somewhere around here and sleep."

"It's pretty cold, darling," I said, getting out stiff and tired and with my stomach growling for food.

"Well, if you're afraid to sleep in the car, I'm not. You can be soft if you want to, but I won't."

"Did I say I wouldn't?" I quickly asked her.

I should have told her to go ahead and sleep out alone. It wouldn't have made any difference in our marriage, and my trying to prove to her that I could play at being a hardy pioneer didn't make her respect me any more, as I shall shortly explain.

"The first thing I want to do is eat," I said. We walked slowly across the road.

"Did you lock the car?" Eloise asked.

"Oh, up here nobody will steal anything."

"Give me the key."

I wasn't thinking of what I was doing or saying, and I handed her the keys. She snatched them out of my hand and rushed across the road and locked the car. I waited for her. I was still getting my bearings, and I guess that I was a little like a man who is just waking up and who isn't at all sure of where he is or what time it is.

A kid of about fifteen came up to me.

"Manger? Eat?" I said.

He said a lot to me in French, but I didn't understand it, and I repeated: *"Manger?* Eat?"

Eloise came back like six wildcats. "My gallant American husband," she said. She didn't exactly say it *to* me. Rather she just about spat out the words *at* me.

"I don't know what he's saying," I said, pointing to the fifteen year old kid.

"Restaurant," he said, pointing ahead of me.

That's what I wanted to hear.

"Albergo," he said, pointing to the building across the road behind us.

"Oui," I said.

I hadn't taken in the scene yet. There was a kind of terrace or platform off a little to my left, and from it you had a wonderful view. I could see that.

"Let's get the view," I said to Eloise. She followed me silently.

I think I ought to add that there was a touch of iciness or of near-iciness in the wind. From this platform you could look down and off. You could see down hundreds and hundreds of kilometers, and down and off for miles. It was nearly dark. The trees were more black than green. Here and there white stone houses looked lonely in the distance, surrounded by the mountains. Just below us, the mountain took a sharp and almost straight decline. Over a distance and on the other side of the decline, was the road we had come up. I could see a small black car, its lights yellow, climbing slowly just as we had climbed a little while before. And between the mountain and the mountain across from us, there was this steep decline, and there was a valley with a few houses, small and white against the night that was coming on, and there was the wind in the trees. The wind was almost inhumanly sad. All of this was beautiful, and I am not ashamed to say that it was. And because it was in another country, not my own, I guess I felt doubly sad. Because an American like myself—I guess I must be pretty typical—who doesn't speak other languages and who doesn't have much culture, well, he can only feel a little bit lost and out of it in Europe, especially when he sees beautiful things, either in nature or the churches and the museums and the castles.

So I stood there on that wooden platform or veranda, and I looked and I listened to the wind in the trees. I was far away from home. Maybe I shouldn't tell you this because it's obvious that I was far away from home, but this was suddenly important to me. I told myself several times that I was far away from home. That is what the wind made me feel. But I kept standing and looking. Tired and hungry as I was, dusty and grimy from the long day on the road, I still didn't want to move. I stood looking because I had the funny idea that something, some idea, was going to come to me that would put everything in my life in place just as if, maybe, my life up to that point had been a jigsaw puzzle with the pieces all mixed up, and now the pieces were all going to be put into their right places, and my life was going to be like a puzzle that was solved or put together.

Do I make sense to you, telling you this? I hope so, because I want to. Here, now, on the boat, I want very much to make sense, and I have a feeling of, well, of nostalgia for that time when I stood looking at the Alps.

Well, in a minute or so, Eloise said to me—and she said it in a pretty cutting way, too—she said: "If you want to freeze and starve, you go ahead, but I'm not going to."

She turned on her heels before I could say anything, and what she had said was like taking the wind out of my sails. Now, I think that that moment was the end, and it was when I really knew everything and knew, that is, that I shouldn't have married her. But I didn't really admit to myself what I knew. I still let myself pretend. I was almost floored. I felt bad. But I turned and tagged after her.

Inside, we found the washrooms and washed and then sat down to eat. The dining room was more than you would expect in a place high up in the Alps. There were pictures on the walls and a number of tables with clean linen tablecloths and genuine sterling silver, too. I'm not particularly observant about the way a room looks and such things, but I liked this place. It was warm, with logs burning in a fireplace, and I'm a sucker for burning logs. I had a feeling of restfulness and of being far away from the world. Suddenly I wasn't lonely because of this, but happy. I wished I could stay right where I was, up in the Alps, for a long time, if not forever. I didn't want to go on. I didn't want to go back to America and pitch into my having a career in the advertising business. Suddenly it seemed as if I had all kinds of things in the world to forget, and I wanted to forget them. I haven't had a really unhappy life, except for my unhappy honeymoon. In a way it was unhappy, but it didn't hit me deeply, my unhappiness. In fact, Eloise's busting out on me didn't cause any deep wounds in me. But sitting there in the dining room of that hotel way up in the Alps, I felt as if I had escaped from all the unhappiness of an unhappy world.

I was sleepy, and I felt some of the warmth of the fireplace. We sipped our drink, *fin a l'eau,* and the liquor was warming. For a few moments it was like living in a dream. And while I had this warm and dreamlike feeling, I thought of how pretty Eloise was. She is a damned pretty girl. With her dark, thick hair and her dark eyes and her round face, she looked so pretty and girlish, so sweet. I wanted to think that all that sweetness of Eloise—

I mean, of course, that sweet-lookingness—all of it was mine. And that all that sweetness loved me. That's what I wanted to feel and believe. Of course, it is not much of a joke to say that in Eloise's case looks were deceiving, but that isn't just a joke. It's the painful truth.

We put away a good meal, steak, and it was cooked almost as well as they cook in France. There weren't many others in the dining room. A young mother playing with a child, a little boy of about two. She was a beautiful and intelligent-looking girl, too. Maybe I am off, but the gals in Europe look as if they were more intelligent than the American girls. This good looker was either French or Swiss. The Swiss speak French as well as German, and this good looker was speaking French to her son. I had a strong impulse. All men have such impulses. I envied that gal's husband. But I didn't look too much at her because Eloise was with me. Now, looking back on my so-called honeymoon, I can see that there were lots, or at least quite a number of little things I didn't do or say or see because of Eloise. And many of them were harmless. I couldn't say giving the eye to a good-looking babe is harmless or harmful. After all, that was the beginning of my so-called marriage. But here I'm not just talking about looking at babes. I'm talking about lots of little things that are harmless without there being any question of a debate or difference of opinion about them.

For instance, there is the matter of seeing something and saying you like it or you don't like it. Take lots of things like pictures or buildings or restaurants or some kind of food, or the way it's cooked or a street or a hotel, and suppose you just happen to like it or not to like it— does it make any difference? Well, sometimes it did, and sometimes it didn't with Eloise. So I just got into the habit of not talking about what I liked or didn't like. I got to thinking about what Eloise would say about what I said before I'd say it, because, hell, we were on a honeymoon, and we were supposed to bill and coo and not fight.

But let me get back to my story. As I said, I ate a good meal. And I had some good red wine, *vin rosé*. The food perked me up a little and I was less tired. And I was feeling so good that all over again I just washed out of

my memory everything unpleasant that had happened between Eloise and myself. We had reached the Alps, and
this should have been our big night—in fact, it should
have been our enchanted night. Wasn't this the night I
had dreamed of all the way across the Atlantic Ocean and
while we had been in Paris? And now it had happened. I
was in the Alps with Eloise. In the morning we could go
over the Colle de Simplon and descend and go on into
Italy. I was pleased with the way I'd driven that Citroën,
and with the distance I'd made. I was kind of thrilled.
Hell, I was thrilled with what I'd seen of the mountains.
I'd had good food and good wine. And Eloise, that pretty
girl sitting across from me, was my wife, my bride.

Of course, now, as the *Queen Mary* nears New York
and I think back on all of this and tell you about it, I
know I was . . . well, sentimental and kind of a fool,
maybe even a damned fool. I'm not sure now if I ever
believed it all and maybe I didn't, but I know I wanted to.
I wanted to believe that everything was going to be wonderful. I guess the way to tell you what I wanted to believe and to have happen to me was that I wanted what
we always call romance to be real, to happen. I wanted the
Alps and Europe to change Eloise and, maybe, to change
me, too.

And as we were eating, I kept hoping that Eloise would
change her mind about sleeping out in the car, but I didn't
bring this subject up for fear that I'd do it in a premature
way or let on to her how much I didn't want to sleep
outside. I just hoped that she would change her mind on
her own; and as we ate, I was watchful for an opening so
that I might introduce the subject in such a way that I
wouldn't rile her up.

Well, telling you all this I suddenly feel kind of foolish.
Maybe I was just a big dope. I was. I was a dope to cater
to Eloise and give her her way.

But to go on with my story. The waitress started talking French to us, and I couldn't get it. Eloise made a show
of understanding, but it was all faking. The waitress—she
wasn't anything at all to write home about—saw that we
didn't savvy what she was saying so she made a switch

to German. That made it worse. And I could see that Eloise was building up to an anger.

"Parlez Française, s'il vous plait," I said to the waitress, but she didn't understand what I was saying until I repeated it three times. So then she speaks French again, and Eloise got the point. The waitress was asking us about our room.

"You tell her you want a room for yourself. I'm sleeping in the car," Eloise said in one of her most sarcastic manners.

I was sunk.

"No, *non,* no room," I told the waitress.

"She doesn't understand English. The phrase is *chambre du lit.*"

So I said no, we didn't want any *chambre du lit.*

Well, we finished our coffee and had a brandy. I still didn't want to move. I didn't like the prospect of going on and finding a place to park the car so that we could sleep out. Of course, I know that this was a romantic thing to do, especially since we were newlyweds. And it could be an adventure. It could, I knew as I sat there sipping my brandy, give us something to talk about to our friends when we got back to America. It would make us seem adventurous, and our friends would even envy us. It would be an experience, or as I have just said, an adventure. And come to think of it, we didn't have many experiences or adventures in Europe. I kept expecting all kinds of things to happen to us, interesting things. I didn't have any clear idea in my mind as to just what these interesting things would be like, but I believed that they would be interesting. And here was something interesting to do, but I didn't want to do it. I didn't want to be rugged and romantic.

And then, too, there was something else which maybe I ought to mention here. I had a passing thought about it at the time. It was this. Here Eloise had been, in one way or another, running me down all during my so-called honeymoon. And now maybe I should have welcomed Eloise's suggestion about sleeping out as an adventure and as a chance to show her and prove that I was adventurous in spirit. But I didn't feel that way. I just wanted a warm, soft, comfortable bed, and I wanted Eloise to be loving with me.

I finished my brandy. I was in for it, and there was nothing to do but go through with it. So reluctantly I paid the bill and we left. It was dark out. The wind was blowing and whistling in the trees, and near us somewhere I could hear a falls or a mountain stream. The moon was lost behind clouds, and just at the bend in the road the trees were tall and black, and the wind was blowing and playing on them. I liked it and I liked the sounds, but it was pretty chilly. For a moment or so, I convinced myself that I'd been all wrong and that I should look forward to the night we had ahead of us.

"Don't worry, you won't get pneumonia."

This kind of flabbergasted me. I didn't get it. Sometimes she'd say something like that, something completely out-of-place, that had no connection with what I'd been saying or thinking about.

Anyway, we got into the car. I took my time in getting set and starting. I had a premonition that it wasn't going to be any fun.

"Why are you so slow?"

"The motor has to be warmed up," I said.

"But you haven't started it yet. Of all the irrelevant people I have ever met, you're the champion."

You can understand from this that we were really getting started off for a truly romantic night in the Alps. And I think I might also add here that I felt, for a minute or so, sitting there at the wheel, just the way I used to feel as a school kid and just about the way that every school kid feels sometimes when he wishes and hopes that the school building will burn down. I wished that the car wouldn't start.

It was slow in warming up, but the engine started and I eased out onto the road, not knowing where we were going and feeling pretty hopeless. I was tired again, too. Just past the hotel and restaurant, the road curved and ascended. There was a clearing there.

"What about here?" I said to Eloise.

"I should think you could pick a space without my having to tell you."

I got sore at this but didn't say anything. I parked the car. It took us an hour, or at least it seemed like an hour, to get the pneumatic mattresses pumped up and the car rigged up for sleeping with the seats down. Then we went to bed.

Now, I'm not going to give you a blow-by-blow account of the night. I'll just tell you enough to give you an idea of what it was like. I might say that I'm rather tall, so I couldn't get myself into a comfortable position, and of course it was really icy. I closed all the windows of the car, but at first Eloise wanted air. A little later, after I reopened one of the car windows, she felt cold too and wanted the window closed. But that wasn't so good either, because the air inside the car was stale.

You can't begin to imagine how many noises there are in the mountains or how many different sounds the wind can make in the trees. And there was the sound of a falls —I saw it the next morning—and what with the wind and the falls making all these noises, Eloise imagined other noises. It was weird, with the two of us uncomfortable and chilled there in the darkness. It seemed like the longest night I ever lived. It seemed like the darkness would last and last, if not forever, then damned near forever. Of course, nothing really happened. I mean, no one attacked us, and we weren't in any danger except perhaps that of getting pneumonia, but fortunately we didn't catch that. But all of this notwithstanding, it did get weird. The darkness and the night seemed to me to be stranger than the darkness and the night had ever been on any other occasion in my life, even when I was a little kid. And with this, there was the chill. And my not being able to get into a comfortable position. And my feeling dirty and dusty from the long day on the road.

And Eloise didn't stand it any better than I did. As a matter of fact, she stood it worse. When we went to bed, if you call that going to bed, she said she was too tired for anything and wanted to go right to sleep. She just about didn't get a wink of sleep all night. And I got scarcely more, because when finally I would start dozing off, Eloise would wake me up to ask me about some noise or sound. Sometimes it had been the noise of the wind in the trees, and maybe once or twice the sound of animals. Or else it was the falls. But she imagined that she heard footsteps and that there were marauders around. And to prove that there must be marauders around, ready to do us harm if not to kill us outright, she spoke about a story that she had read in the Paris edition of the *Herald Tribune,* telling of how an Englishman and his family had been killed while sleeping in their car somewhere on the French Riviera near Nice. I tried to calm her by saying that Nice and the French Riviera were far, far away from us. But this only got her sore, and at last it gave me the creeps, too.

I'd be just dozing off, thinking that this time I was really going to sleep, and then, in a low and frightened voice, Eloise would ask me: "What's that?"

How did I know what that was when it was, as likely as not, nothing but a figment of Eloise's imagination? Now, all of this, with the chilliness, it was . . . well, it was just damned uncomfortable and not the least bit romantic. And then along about or near the time when the dawn would be coming up—but I didn't know that because my watch stopped and so did Eloise's and so did the clock on the dashboard—along about the time when the dawn would start creeping over the mountains and through this pitch darkness, when I was numbed with cold, Eloise blamed me for all her misery.

"This was your idea," she said at me in an angry voice.

"What was my idea?" I asked, very sleepily and only half-located.

"This. Do you mean to deny it?"

"Honey, I want to sleep, so please let's not . . ."

She didn't let me finish. "You can sleep like an ox now, but I have to freeze to death."

"Let me warm you up."

"After lying to my face, don't you dare touch me."

"Oh . . ." I exclaimed, letting out a big, wide, noisy yawn.

"I hate you!"

She said this as if she had meant it and now, remembering it, I am inclined to believe that she really did mean it.

I sat up straight. "What the hell's the matter, Eloise?" I asked her, trying to rub some of the sleep out of my eyes.

She came out with it and said that sleeping out in the car like this had been my idea of being romantic, and that it was my fault that she was almost frozen to death. Now, when she said this, I got sore. I got sore as hell, and I was hurt because what Eloise said and accused me of just wasn't so, and it was so damned unfair.

"What the hell are you talking about?"

"You know what I'm talking about. You just about made me do this—all because you wanted to play at being romantic, just as though you were Lord Byron."

"That ain't so. You wanted to do this."

"You can lie that way to my face?"

By now the dawn was coming. It was getting gray. You could see more and more of the shapes and outlines of the trees, and you could see the houses on the other side of the road. And we sat there fighting like cats and dogs as to whose idea it had been for us to sleep in the car. And I couldn't get her to admit or to remember that she and not I had insisted on doing this. I kept trying to, but my efforts only made her all the more furious, and all the choice names she called me aren't worth repeating. I'd never seen her like this before. She was like a cat ready to spit. And after my getting sore myself, my anger cooled off, and I wanted to stop the fight. But she wouldn't. She still insisted that I admit that sleeping in the car in the Alps had been my idea, not hers. That I wouldn't admit, because it wasn't true. You can see that it wasn't true from the story I told you.

Well, that's my story. I finally got out of the car in the chilly dawn, and Eloise got out after me, still fighting mad, still demanding that I admit what wasn't true—to wit, that it had all been my idea and my fault. And because I reared on my hind legs, so to speak, I wouldn't give in to her. We took a little walk along a path that led to the falls we'd heard all night. With the sun coming up, it was a splendid, wonderful sight, but we were too busy fighting to enjoy and appreciate it. I was as . . . yes, well, shocked as I was sore, because Eloise was steadfast in her denial that it had been her desire, not mine, to sleep in the car. I couldn't understand this, and I still can't. Hell, if I'd have known or guessed that Eloise was going to spring anything like this on me, I'd have let her sleep alone in the car.

And that's what happened. If I tried to tell you what she said at any length, all I'd be doing is to tell you the many ways she thought up to insult me.

She kept it up at breakfast, too. We sat outside at the café in the chilly air, but it kept getting warmer with the sun up. I thought how nice and pleasant a breakfast we might have had, talking and having our coffee and sending postcards to friends back home in America. But it wasn't anything like that. A bus stopped in front of us. It was a big blue one, with a little trailer wagon connected behind. Mail and packages were in the trailer. The day before, I had passed buses like this; some of them, going the other way, had passed me, and I'd wondered what the trailers were for. I watched the mountain people get on the bus and noticed the big hobnailed shoes they were wearing and saw a few others pass by on foot, and I saw the cars pass, and the sun was getting warmer, and I saw all of the signs of it turning into a wonderful day. And Eloise jawed at me.

We finally set off for Italy, but Eloise didn't say much and I didn't either. It was rotten, going along with us both sore at one another, and her so heated up. We got to Milan by two-thirty, and just like that, without warning, she said she was through with me. And I guess she meant it, because I left her at a hotel and she had the hotel get her a ticket by train back to Paris.

Now she's in New York, and I'll be home tomorrow. I don't think I want to see her. I don't know what I want to do. I don't know if I'd ever like to see the Alps again. But I guess I've got nothing more to say except that now, if I remember the Alps, I think of it just being so cold there because of the night we spent, sleeping out in that Citroën.